A Compromising Passion

Nell Kincaid

Thorndike Press • Chivers Press
Waterville, Maine USA Bath, England

This Large Print edition is published by Thorndike Press®, USA
and by Chivers Press, England.

Published in 2003 in the U.S. by arrangement with Maureen Moran Agency.

Published in 2003 in the U.K. by arrangement with the author.

U.S. Softcover 0-7862-5389-4 (Paperback Series)
U.K. Hardcover 0-7540-7232-0 (Chivers Large Print)
U.K. Softcover 0-7540-7233-9 (Camden Large Print)

The text of this Large Print edition is unabridged.
Other aspects of the book may vary from the original edition.

Set in 16 pt. Plantin by Liana M. Walker.

Printed in the United States on permanent paper.

British Library Cataloguing-in-Publication Data available

Library of Congress Cataloging-in-Publication Data

Kincaid, Nell.
A compromising passion / Nell Kincaid.
p. cm.
ISBN 0-7862-5389-4 (lg. print : sc : alk. paper)
1. Theatrical agents — Fiction. 2. Baseball players — Fiction. 3. Large type books. I. Title.
PS3561.I42533C66 2003
813′.6—dc21 2003042658

A Compromising Passion

CHAPTER ONE

"Ex-First Baseman in Centerfold — Is Nothing Sacred?"

Andrea Sutton laughed and quickly skimmed the angry editorial about her next client, Jim Haynes. He had incurred the wrath — and admiration — of thousands of people when he had posed for a nude centerfold in *Fantasies* magazine. Everyone from angry fans to lovestruck readers had written to him. Everyone, that is, except Hollywood and New York casting directors — the very people whose attention he'd sought.

Andrea could well imagine what had happened, for the same thing happened to hundreds of people every day. Jim Haynes, ex-first baseman for the New York Aces, a major-league team, wanted to be an actor. And even though he was probably savvy in a hundred other areas, he knew nothing about show business. Which was where Andrea came in.

Imagine, she thought to herself. Who would have imagined that the Jim Haynes she had pined for from afar all through high school would ever come to her for anything?

Theirs had been a classic situation: he was the handsome and popular jock at a large Long Island school, she was quiet and shy; he dated blond cheerleaders, heads of social committees, prom queens; she dated people nobody had ever heard of, when she dated at all. For even though she was pretty and smart, somehow she seemed to fade into the background when functions like dances came up. And people like Jim Haynes were always at the forefront, laughing and having the kind of great time everyone else in school dreamed of.

Normally he would have been the kind of guy she didn't even like: he was too popular, too good-looking, too all-around perfect to be interesting. Only somehow he was different from the boys who emulated him, the boys some girls settled for when they couldn't get dates with Jim.

Andrea had always sensed this, and then one day she knew she had been right. She was in school late one afternoon, sitting in the cubicle at the end of the third-floor hallway, reading. As one of the editors of the school literary magazine, she checked the cubicle every afternoon to see what had been submitted for consideration. And today when she had come in, her heart nearly stopped. There in the slotted cardboard box was one submission: "Memories of an Afternoon," by James T. Haynes.

Andrea could remember the story even now — a moving, gentle, apparently autobiographical story of a young man spending an afternoon with an old blind man in the park. The setting seemed suspiciously like the suburban Long Island town in which Andrea and Jim lived, and the young man seemed very much like the quiet side of Jim that Andrea had hoped existed.

But she had never finished the story because Jim had come in just as she was halfway through, and had asked for it back.

"Why?" she had asked boldly. Shy as she was, this little cubicle was her domain.

"I don't want anything in the magazine," he had said quietly.

All at once she had understood. He couldn't let this wonderful story about a vulnerable and sensitive high-school kid be published in the school magazine. Jim Haynes was a softball star, a great date, a superb distance runner — the kind of guy every other guy in high school wanted to be like. How could *that* Jim Haynes have written this story?

Andrea hoped this might be her big chance: she'd gracefully show Jim that she understood, and he'd . . . But as she looked at him, she knew nothing would happen. He was too handsome, with his dark blue eyes and brown hair, too popular, too perfect to let anything happen.

And she had been right. He had thanked her and left, and that was the beginning, middle, and end of their relationship.

But there was about to be a new beginning. She was about to become his personal manager, to launch him on the acting career he wanted to begin now that an arm injury had permanently forced him out of baseball.

Andrea looked at the large pictures of some of her clients on the wall — blown-up magazine covers, fashion layouts, stills from recent films. Many of them had started out by paying to have their photographs taken for portfolios; now their faces were everywhere, recognized by everyone. And Andrea had had a great part in putting each and every one of them on the map.

The intercom on Andrea's desk buzzed, and when her secretary said, "Jim Haynes is here," she was suddenly as nervous as when Jim had found her in the cubicle all those years before. As if no time had passed, he was the popular guy who was completely unattainable, totally beyond reach. And she was the painfully shy, dark-haired girl who could admire him and think about him and know him only from afar, except in her dreams and fantasies.

The door opened, and Jim Haynes walked in. Andrea didn't even hear Rachelle make the introductions; she didn't even see her leave. All she saw was a dark-haired figure who had grown from boy to man since she had last seen him, who was smiling at her as if they had always been the best of friends.

She had studied his pictures over the years, of course, but most had been in newspapers — fuzzy and flat and black-and-white. None had captured the deep blue of those dark-lashed eyes, the irresistible persuasion of his grin, the luster of his dark wavy hair.

"You look fantastic, Andrea," he said, stepping forward as she rose from her chair. His voice had deepened and grown leathery, thick, husky. And from his eyes shone a humor that had been absent in high school.

"It's good to see you, Jim," she said, taking his hand in hers. She smiled. "I've seen you so many times on TV, but it *has* been a long time."

He grinned. "Are you a fan?"

"Sure. I'd have a season ticket if I had time to go, but I think I've been to a game exactly once in the last five years."

"Really?" he said, looking at her curiously. The blue of his eyes was mesmerizing, taking her back in time once again. . . . "I don't remember seeing you at any of the games in high school."

She laughed. "Yes. Well. I wasn't in the cheerleading set. And actually . . ." She smiled.

"What?" he asked, tilting his head.

"Well, I would have liked to have gone to more games, but I would have been a little embarrassed to have anyone see me there."

"What?" He was fighting a smile, but she thought she could see some hurt in his eyes as well. "Why?"

"Hey, listen, I thought cheerleaders were girls who were only interested in good times with the jocks. At the time I didn't think any of you could even read or write. I thought I was going to write the Great American Novel, so I couldn't be seen at anything as unintellectual — and fun — as a softball game."

He laughed. "Well, I'm glad you came once in a while. And now I'm glad I came today." His eyes swept over her face. "No thanks to all the fights I had with my agent. I just didn't want another manager."

"Mmm. I heard about that. Why don't we sit down though?"

In addition to Andrea's desk — walnut with mother-of-pearl geometric inlays — there was a long low burgundy Brazilian leather couch and two matching chairs in one corner of the office, a bank of TV screens set into the opposite wall, with a complete bar set into the wall to the left of the monitors. When Sloan Hammond, Andrea's partner, had first shown her the office he had had redecorated for her, she had felt it was absurdly lavish, like a TV version of what a "glamorous" office should look like. But she had soon learned that everything in it was absolutely necessary — the monitors and video-cassette recorders so that she could review her clients' and prospective clients' work and the fully stocked bar for all her guests. It was a comfortable room in which everyone could feel as relaxed as possible. And, perhaps most important of all, she had to create an atmosphere of extreme luxury, an aura of such success that everyone who walked through the doors of her office would want to be touched by that success in some way. As Sloan Hammond had said to her when she had first begun working as his assistant six years before, "You would hardly put your career in the hands of a man with a seedy one-room office in the West Forties now, would you? What you're going to learn with me over and over and over again, Andrea, is that *hype* is not a dirty word, that the illusion of success quite often brings real success, and that there's nothing wrong with manipulating the truth in order to get your client the recognition he's hired you to produce."

Now, though, as Andrea sat beside Jim on the couch, it was all she could do to make herself concentrate on the fact that he was even her client; as far as her emotions were concerned, he was still Jim Haynes, Mr. Unattainable. Yet coupled with this sameness from the past was the strangeness over the fact that he was a man now, not a boy; it was a man who was sitting next to her in a deep-blue velour pullover and black corduroy pants, a man whose voice had a huskiness that reached her somewhere deep inside, a man who leaned back and spread his arms behind him and smiled that provocative smile she had forgotten about. "So do you have big plans for me? Are you going to make me a star?" he asked half-jokingly.

"A lot of that's up to you," she said.

"Eighty-five percent, would you say?"

She laughed. "Are you unhappy with the fifteen percent we take?"

"Is that a hint that you'll take less?"

"Definitely not! Listen — for what we do, fifteen percent is standard to low. I've heard of a lot of fifty-fifty splits lately between managers and their clients."

He smiled but said nothing, his blue eyes sparkling with challenge, daring her to say more.

"What are you smiling at?" she asked.

"You. I'd heard you were the best in the business. The name Andrea Sutton came up every time I asked anyone about management. And for a week or so I just didn't connect the name with you. When I finally realized . . ." He shook his head. "That quiet Andrea Sutton from Hamilton High. Did the assistant editor of *The Muse* ever think she'd be a personal manager?"

Her green eyes flickered with interest; she was surprised he remembered. And then, as she saw the pleasure in his eyes, she suspected he *didn't* really remember; somehow he had dredged the information out of something other than his memory.

"As a matter of fact," he went on, "weren't you also planning to be a dancer? You gave a couple of really great performances for the junior and senior projects."

Andrea reddened at the memory of her performances: she had been so nervous that she had forgotten half the movements she had choreographed. Nobody but her dance teacher and a few of her friends had known, but even so . . . And then something clicked: junior and senior projects — modern dance. The words sounded suspiciously like her yearbook blurb. . . .

"You rat!" she cried. "Here I am, amazed at the details you've remembered from twelve or thirteen years ago. And then I realize," she said slowly, meeting his mischievous deep blue gaze.

"Realize what? I have nothing to hide."

"Mmm. Right. Listen — you're going to have to hone your acting skills about a thousand percent if you're going to be my client. 'Yes, I've read the yearbook' is written all over your face."

He grinned. "So I've been caught. But it's guilty with an explanation, Andrea."

"Oh, really?" she asked skeptically, trying to suppress a smile.

"Yes, really. I wanted to make a good impression. Since we didn't know each other in high school, I figured there might be things I have to make up for." He shrugged. "So I thought I'd start by acting as if I had known you better than . . . well, better than I guess I did." His dark blue eyes met hers. "Funny — looking at you now I would have thought we would have known each other."

"Uh-uh," she objected, smiling and shaking her head. "Absolutely no way, Jim, because you were a strictly blond-hair-and-blue-eyes man. Or boy."

He slowly shook his head. "You're right," he mused. "Jerk that I was. I hate looking back on those years — all that high-school business."

"Why? I would have thought you'd like to look back."

"Nah," he said. "I think I resent those years because they made me feel everything would be that easy. And nothing *was* once I left high school. All of a sudden I was one of a thousand kids in the freshman class in college, and I hated it." He shrugged. "I'm embarrassed to admit that I cared that much about all that adulation, but I really did get used to it in high school."

She looked at him carefully, letting his blue eyes cast their old spell. She had always been wary of the client who was too obsessed with the public, too easily wounded by bad reviews or difficult interviews. And she realized she didn't know how strong Jim would be when his career was buffeted by unexpected people and events. "I don't want to ask you why you've decided to go into acting, Jim, because I don't think it really matters — and you could have a wonderful and interesting reason and still be unable to put it into words. But I do want to ask you whether you think you're really ready for all that we hope will come in the near future. It's not going to be all fan letters and six-figure contracts."

"Hey, I know that, Andrea. I spent two years in the minors and got sent down three times in the next two years, and I knew, just like every other player knows, that it could happen anytime they wanted to make it happen."

"But you would get sent down only if you did something wrong, and —"

"That wasn't always true," he interrupted. "You could be brought in to the major leagues because another player — the guy you were replacing — was hurt, and once he got better, you could get bumped even if you *weren't* screwing up."

"Well, okay, I see your point," she said. "But acting and this whole image-making thing is very different. So much depends on chance and so much can be taken away so quickly. How many times have you read about TV stars who gave up their roles in very successful series because they thought they'd have greater success in their own series or in the movies?"

"I can think of a few," he began.

"Well, let me tell you: there are dozens, maybe hundreds. There've got to be people I don't know about too. And one of the reasons I don't know about a lot of them is that they've failed — *for no explicable reason.* Their acting hasn't gotten worse; their looks haven't changed; they haven't even changed managers. Half the time their new film or series is better than what they were in before, so you can't blame the script or the person's costars. Something has happened, that's all."

He stared. " 'Something has happened'?" he repeated incredulously. "I pay you fifteen percent to guide and analyze my career and a time might come when you'll tell me 'Something happened'?"

"Let's hope not. But it might. Look, Jim, anyone who professes to know all the answers in this business is a liar. And I want you to try to be ready for unexpected turns."

"I know of one unexpected turn already," he said softly.

"What's that?"

"I never thought I'd be as happy with my decision to hire you as I am. My friends had to struggle for days to get me to agree. But something told me to say yes. And I'll tell you something, Andrea, all that stuff you said about chance in show business — that's true in baseball too. Hell, I couldn't analyze why I hit beautifully in one game and struck out in another. Some players pretend they can, but they really can't. And I'm glad you're being honest. And I want you to know why I want to go into acting."

She smiled. "Okay, why?"

"Because nothing has ever given me that thrill — the same thrill I'd get at home plate, the same rush of adrenaline I'd get when I knew the swing was great, when I heard the crack of the ball, when I took off and felt as if I were the wind. Nothing compared to that until I started acting. And don't laugh, but it was for that small part I had in *Tomorrow and Forever.* I had one or two lines. But when those cameras started to roll, I felt like a million dollars and I thought, This is it. This is what's going to make me feel as good as I did when I was playing." He smiled. "I know other guys've had thousands of arguments with their wives: Don't I make you feel as good as the game does? the wives would always ask, and the guys all say Yes, dear, but when you come right down to it, at least half of them are lying. Which is too bad, but at least they've got *some*thing — the game. And a lot of guys — and women — in this world have nothing. So I just feel damned lucky I've had a career that's made me as happy as it did — and that I might have a chance to have another that could be as good. And who knows? Maybe in my personal life things will pick up too. If I succeed as an actor, I mean." His eyes met hers. "I was in with a handful of guys on my team that weren't married, and we used to get more flack for that." He laughed and shook his head. "Some of those days were really wild. And it's sad, really, because those guys who were married used to say, 'Hey, Jim, really; settle down. It's the only way —' Half those guys are divorced now, with their wives writing books about how all-out rotten it was to be a baseball wife."

"And was it?"

"Hell, yes. *I* think so. Which is one reason I never wanted to put anyone through that. And I'm not ready now either. But that doesn't mean I want things to be as difficult as they were when I broke up with my last girlfriend." He shrugged, and Andrea saw a flash of sadness — regret, perhaps — in his dark blue eyes. "Well, I guess you don't need to hear all about *that.* And I guess I should learn not to be so talkative, huh? For interviews, I mean."

She sighed. It was so refreshing to hear someone speak as candidly as Jim had that she was loath to say anything even slightly negative. As he spoke he seemed totally consumed by what he was saying, completely unaware that he was going on for longer than most people would ever consider doing with someone they weren't close to. He seemed willing to expose his emotions, which was a quality she considered important in her friends and essential in her clients. The only problem was that Jim would have to learn not to "tell all" at the asking of one simple question.

"We'll go over all that later," she finally

said. "I'll arrange every interview you have, so we'll go over what you'll say in each before they actually happen, and —" He was frowning. "What's the matter?"

"I just don't know if I like that idea, that's all. I mean, hell — I know I talk too much some of the time, but isn't that up to me?"

"Well, no, not if you want me to do my job."

He leaned back and stared. "But what if I were being interviewed by someone who looked like you? I'd forget everything I was supposed to say anyway."

She laughed. "Come on."

"I'm serious. I'm still trying to figure out why I didn't really know you in high school."

"Well, maybe I just didn't go out with your type, okay?"

"What about now?"

"Now?" She was suddenly self-conscious, once again tongue-tied and in a haze.

"What type do you go out with now?"

"No type at all, I hope. Just . . . whomever I happen to like."

He raised a brow. "That sounds pretty casual. Anything serious?"

She shook her head, a dark lock of hair

falling over her eyes. "No, not at the moment," she said quietly.

"Don't tell me I've seen you at one of those bars in my neighborhood — ?"

"What bars are those?"

"Singles bars. I live in the heart of the bar scene, fortunately or unfortunately, depending on how you look at it."

"The East Side?"

He nodded.

"Hmm." She smiled. "I'm at Seventy-first and First. What about you?"

"Four blocks away," he said, his lips curving into a grin. "But you still haven't answered my question. Are you a, shall we say, frequenter of that scene?"

"Shall we say neither yes nor no? I really don't discuss my private life with clients, Jim."

"Ah. But you discuss *theirs*."

"Of course. I have to."

"But we're old friends, Andrea."

"Oh, come on. Not really. I was one of hundreds of girls you *didn't* know at Hamilton High because we weren't cheerleaders, and you were someone I knew only at a distance."

"Except for one afternoon," he said quietly, his azure eyes darkening at the memory. "And I can even remember what you were wearing that day, Andrea."

She was stunned. Utterly astonished. Jim Haynes? Mr. Popularity? Why on earth would he have remembered what she was wearing?

"Don't look so surprised. You made quite an impression on me. After all those years, I didn't remember your name last week, but if someone had said the girl who gave you back your story, I could have told them everything about that afternoon."

"But why?"

"You were so different from everyone I knew. So quiet — just sitting in that little room, reading, and you were wearing all black. I thought, This girl could never in a million years have a conversation with Cindi McGhee." He smiled. "Remember her?"

"Your girlfriend? Sure. She blackballed a friend of mine in college when my friend wanted to get into a sorority house and Cindi didn't want anyone from her past around."

"Mmm. A real sweetie. She was looking for a tutor for her English class, I remember. And I thought, This girl could do it, but I'm only going to ask her one favor. I thought you looked like a writer or something."

She laughed. "I would have been thrilled if you had told me even half of that."

"Well, I was concentrating on just one thing, and that was getting my story back."

She looked at him and wondered how his life might have been different if he hadn't been channeled so early into being a sports hero. Certainly he loved baseball, and he was one of those lucky few in the world who are able to work at something they love and get paid for it. But she had seen a different side of him that day back in high school. He was no longer Mr. Popularity, the boy with more dates than others could dare to dream of, the one who was always laughing, smiling, waving as the crowd cheered. He was sensitive, even uncertain. And now, with his interest in acting, he seemed to try to be combining the two parts of his life. Yet he had hidden — since before that day he had taken his story back — his more vulnerable side.

"Why was it so important? Getting it back, I mean."

"Oh, you knew the answer then and you know it now. That wasn't my image and I didn't want my image to change. I was really happy then."

"What about changing your image

now?" she asked, gesturing at the open folder full of clippings. "Your friend Owen did a beautiful job of making you out as a very, well, almost like a caricature of the easygoing, lady-killing but mindless ball player. Real beefcake — a real hunk. So my job with you is different from what it is with most clients, because you're already famous. And if you want to change your image, my job is that much harder: we've got to change the public's mind rather than just present them with someone interesting."

"Look," he said quietly, his leathery voice suddenly hoarser than usual. "I'm really glad to be working with you, Andrea, but what's so wrong with what Owen did? I mean, hell — I've got my complaints about him — he was a liar for one thing, and a thief for another. But most of that image stuff is true." He grinned. "Embarrassing but true."

She glanced down at an article that had appeared in a Cleveland, Ohio, paper. "Haynes and Co. Back in Town — Watch Out!" She raised a brow. "Yes. Well, no one expects or wants their movie heroes to be choirboys or monks. But you do have to start acting more serious. And I know that that probably sounds silly or worse. But think about directors and casting agents — it's not that you can't be a hell-raiser some of the time or even all of the time. But you can't be thought of as a joker, as a guy who shouldn't be cast in anything more dramatic than beer commercials. And that's where it'll be important to choose the parts you audition for very carefully, and to at least *try* to turn the image away from the *Fantasies* centerfold, Mr. February, or whatever you were."

He laughed. "April. The cruelest month, right? I know it was for me, anyway." He shook his head. "I still haven't heard the end of that, and it's been over six months! Every time I go into Jason's on First Avenue — or any place where the players hang out — I hear centerfold jokes for the first half hour I'm there." His eyes met hers. "So you saw it?"

She reddened. *Damn it,* she thought. *You're thirty years old and you're not supposed to let anything make you blush.* Except that the memory of that picture did just that, especially when the real version of that magnificent man was sitting next to her.

She didn't usually buy *Fantasies* magazine. She plowed through so many magazines that were important in her work that she had absolutely no time to indulge in reading anything else. And the quality of the magazine had never been that great anyway. But when she saw the words "April's Fantasy: Gorgeous Hunk First Baseman Jim Haynes," she practically ripped the magazine out of the newsstand rack.

And she had found the picture incredibly arousing, an image she couldn't shake from her thoughts, day or night, for weeks. She had always, of course, found him handsome. His dark wavy hair and steel-blue eyes had always held a special fascination for her. But in the centerfold series he had roused her to a new appreciation of him. In the main picture he was stretched out in a magnificent, cathedral-ceilinged lodge, raised up on one elbow, with one leg stretched out and the other bent at the knee. The pose had shown off his magnificent chest, muscled and covered with fine dark hair, and his long lean legs, clearly made of sheer power made strong from years of sports. His was the kind of body kisses were meant to rain on, that could be loved over and over again. And she had looked at it often.

She shook herself out of the heat of

memory and said, "Yes, I saw it back when it came out."

For a moment he looked embarrassed, his dark lashes shading his eyes in a way she remembered as very appealing in high school. And then he grinned. "Part of your work as a dedicated talent scout?"

"Of course. What other reason could I possibly have had? The fact that I knew you in high school and that your name was about a foot high on the cover had nothing to do with it."

He smiled, but the smile was brief, and a moment later he leaned forward, hung his hands between his knees, and slowly shook his head. "What you said about those casting directors. You think it'll hurt my chances?"

She was thinking of the picture again. How many other women had been unable to exorcise the image of Jim from their minds? How many other women had imagined making love with him, running their lips along his hard thighs, giving him the pleasure he was so obviously designed to give and receive?

"Do you?" he asked quietly.

"What? Oh, no, no. I really don't think so. They'll see you can obviously . . ." But words left her. What could she say?

"Play nude love scenes?" he asked almost innocently.

"Well. Whatever. You're obviously leading-man material."

"Ah. Good."

"Did you get lots of letters, by the way?"

"You mean after the centerfold? Surprisingly, yes. The magazine forwarded them by the sack. Owen was talking about doing a poster."

"Well, you can forget about that for now," she said firmly.

"Why?"

"Weren't you just asking me if the centerfold would hurt your chances?"

"Yes, but —"

"Well, I don't see why it would. That was six months ago, and it was a lark. But a poster would put you right back into the category of another run-of-the-mill athlete-turned-actor. You could get parts as a baseball player, maybe a quarterback, a sportscaster — all the parts that sports figures get because they've been typecast. It would be the first step on the wrong road that would lead people to believe you'd do anything for publicity and nothing that has any inherent value. You want to act; it's my job to help you get the parts that will do you some good, and *then* to develop your image in a large-scale way. So let me worry about poster deals and things like that in the future."

He said nothing, and looked as if he had barely been listening. She wondered if he had tuned out because he was annoyed by what she was saying.

But then he said, "Tell me something. Why — how are you so sure of what you're saying? I'm ready to accept what you say, but still — something just nags at me."

"I don't think you *are* ready to accept it, actually. You keep *saying* you're ready — every time you object to something I've told you. And I'm used to it; no one likes being told what to do, and I can tell you right now that the feeling will get stronger rather than weaker."

"Oh, great. But I don't believe that. If I see you're doing a great job —"

"You'll resent me," she interrupted. "I don't want to give you a big speech about what a thankless job this is, but let me warn you — our relationship is going to go way downhill at some point, and probably when you least expect it."

"What are you? A psychologist?" he demanded. "Even if you were, what makes you so sure? I may not have remembered the name Andrea Sutton but I remembered *you.* And what I remembered, I liked. What I've seen today, I like more. So don't you go telling me that our relationship is going to do *anything* that you don't know for a fact."

"Look — I've had a lot of experience in this area, Jim. I've worked with Sloan for six years now, and I've watched a lot of other managers over the years too. And almost invariably the relationship between the client and the manager gets very tense and very unpleasant. I had one client whose name I can't tell you. It was a very sad, very classic case. He started to believe his own publicity and to feel he didn't need me, and to resent me for the role I had played in his success. I don't like it when that happens, no matter how predictable it may be. I still care about the person, I'm still proud of the job I've done, and I don't like the kind of rotten treatment he gave me. He ended up firing me too."

"What happened then? Tell me who he is."

She shook her head. "I really can't. He *was* very famous. He's not anymore. Or rather, his name is still well-known, but it won't be for long because he doesn't get any work. When he started to turn sour on me, he turned sour on everyone else, and he was sometimes absolutely impossible to work with, so everyone decided it was easier not to take the chance. He panicked and started drinking again, and then there was no question about whether he would be impossible on the set; everyone knew he would be." Her eyes met Jim's. "Now, I'm not saying he failed because I was no longer his manager; my role is important, but there certainly have been thousands of people who have succeeded without managers."

"So what *are* you saying?" Jim asked a bit testily.

She sighed. "I was telling you how relationships in this business go downhill fast, even when business is going beautifully. This man I'm telling you about, he didn't fight with me and resent me when we were struggling with his career, *then* he appreciated my help. But when he was on top of the world he felt he could get rid of everyone who had been with him at the beginning. He didn't want to be reminded of the fact that we had helped him and he hadn't done it on his own."

"Are you saying that's what's going to happen to me?" He looked at her in amazement. "I can't believe you think you're such a seer. I know you have to be self-confident in your work, but come on!"

"Look," she said firmly. "I do know what I'm talking about. There's a saying in this business that if you really succeed, you have to either fire or marry your manager. And it's true enough to keep it in mind."

"You don't seem too worried about the other possibility. The marriage one."

"Oh, as far as I know, that's never happened with woman managers — only with female clients and male managers."

He raised a brow. "Interesting. What do you think that means?"

She shrugged. "I think it's fairly simple. The Svengali role is okay if a man is doing it, if Daddy tells his little girl what to do. But the other way around — that's a turnoff rather than a turn-on I think."

"That's just insecurity when people can't take advice. Ballplayers are used to it though. We've got managers, coaches, owners, other players, everyone telling us what to do. And in the end the only smart way to go is to do what you think is right — but you don't go crazy if people offer you some advice."

She shook her head. "Sorry. We'll work together, obviously. But if I'm going to earn my fifteen percent, you've got to trust me."

"What about trusting *me?* We knew each

other in high school, but already you've put up a barrier as if we'd never known each other, telling me you won't discuss your private life as if I'm a stranger. I'm interested, and I'm not going to pretend we never knew each other."

She smiled. "Here you go with this high school business again! I think it's sweet of you to pretend we knew each other, but we didn't except for that one day, and —"

"And we never will?" he asked softly. "I've been sitting here wishing I had said more that day when you gave me back my story. Are you saying I'm not going to have that chance?"

"Obviously we'll know each other," she said, meeting his gaze. "And don't forget I *do* know you: I remember how you went out with ten different girls at a time, and I see from your clippings that your reputation hasn't changed one bit. So if this is the smooth Jim Haynes approach I remember hearing about" — and *wishing for,* she added silently — "save it for the parts I'm going to help you get."

He smiled. "But I like you," he said. There was a suggestion of self-mockery in his tone, as if he knew that he was being presumptuous, that he was suggesting that if he liked her, that was all that mattered.

But there was also a commanding confidence beneath, an instinct that apparently told him she wanted him.

As he drew closer, she half felt as if she were in a dream, a dream like so many she had had back in school.

He was going to kiss her; she could feel it in every part of her body, feel the fire she knew his touch would ignite, feel the pulse pounding inside.

She was caught by the moment, suspended in wonder and desire as he gathered her in his arms, touched by magic as his lips lightly brushed against hers. At that first meeting of their lips they raised their eyes to each other and then smiled, just briefly. Surprise and wonder slipped deeper into pleasure as he covered her mouth with his, and her lips parted as he entered its sweetness. Her reaction was immediate — a heated, blissful haze through which she could only dimly wonder how it could be so good so fast, an urgency that grew as he deepened the kiss. He pulled her on top of him and enveloped her in his strong arms, exploring her back and the curves of her hips and buttocks with his warm hands, sending surging warmth through every part of her body.

She tore her mouth from his and drew

back in confusion, wanting to get another look at the eyes of the man who could reach her so quickly. His eyes were stormy with lust, heavy-lidded and dark, and with sighs they fell into each other's arms again. He kissed her neck and nuzzled in the softness of her hair, gently grazed her earlobe and teased inside with the tip of his warm tongue. And all the while, as she was loving the firm strength of his back beneath her fingers, and the hardness of his buttocks, she thought, *Maybe it's because he was a fantasy for so long. Maybe it's because that picture brought back all those memories.* Maybe it was because at some level, she knew he had been the fantasy object of hundreds of thousands of women but he was kissing her. Whatever the reason, though, she felt as if she were on fire, as if she could kiss him forever, as if she had been made for him and him alone.

For a moment she remembered that this was the office, that anyone could walk in. *You didn't plan to do this.* But when he claimed her lips with his once again she couldn't resist the heat, the moans that drew them closer, the instinctive need to get closer to his hard male frame.

He drew back and smiled. "I think that was definitely worth a twelve-year wait.

Hell, Andrea, if I had known you kissed like that in high school, I would have asked you out every night of the week."

She looked at him skeptically. "For your information I *didn't* kiss like that in high school. I hardly went out at all because all the guys like you ignored the 'brains' and everyone who was anything but a prom queen or a pompom girl."

He shook his head. "Big, big mistake on my part," he murmured.

"Well, actually, this . . . wasn't exactly a *mistake,* but it's not something I do with clients, and I realize I said that before, but I do mean it."

"Not kissing in the office, you mean? I think other places can be arranged."

She shook her head. "You know what I mean."

He frowned. "Office rule?"

"My rule. I can go out with whomever I want. But because of all those things I told you before — how difficult the relationships between me and my clients can get — I like to try to keep things simple."

"But you make exceptions? It's up to you rather than some boss of yours."

She smiled. "I don't have a boss. Sloan and I are partners. And I made the rule for myself." She thought of the kiss they had just shared — that magical moment in which their lips had promised so much, their tongues had danced in a frenzy of wild desire. There was something very appealing about this new development, about the fact that Jim Haynes wanted to go out with her.

But there were so many reasons not to. There was the reason she had told him, which was a valid one. Sound and logical. And one she would forget about in a minute if it weren't for the most important one of all — Jim himself.

In high school, even at those times when she wanted him most, when she used to take major detours just to get a glance at him, she had known deep inside that he wasn't for her, that he would hurt her in the end, that nothing more than a few dates could ever be possible. Now, having had what she felt was more than her share of experience with men like Jim, she could spot him and others of his type almost immediately. He was too good-looking, too accustomed to taking advantage, too used to success with women as well as in other areas of his life. Things came easily to men of his type. Which was fine, except at age thirty, Andrea was old enough to spot Jim Haynes as someone who could really hurt her. He had a deep effect on her even now, after all these years. He was strictly a love-'em-and-leave-'em guy. He spelled danger.

But it was easier to blame it on work; the last thing she wanted was to get into a detailed airing of her real feelings.

He reached out and touched her arm, his rough hand warm against the smooth skin of her upper arm. And when he gently trailed downward, Andrea's memory of their kiss smoldered deep inside.

"I'll do my best to do what you want," he said huskily, "but I can't make any promises I'll stay away from you."

She smiled. "Oh, come on. You waited twelve years."

"I hadn't kissed you," he said, bringing his thumb down to bear on the crease in her elbow. "How am I going to stop thinking about what happened here this afternoon?" he asked, smiling.

"Oh, I'm sure you'll find a way," she answered, pulling away from his grasp as she stood up. The room was suddenly too hot, too close. She walked around to her desk and flipped open her appointment book. "Let's set something up for a few days from now, okay? After the weekend."

He stood up and walked slowly over to where she stood, on her side of the desk.

"Are you avoiding me?" There was a glint of mischief in his eye, but an edge of seriousness roughened the undertones of his voice.

"I'm trying to set up our next appointment, okay?" She winced over the way her words had come out. Her voice was shaky. its strength buried under layers of uncertainty. She had to avoid his eyes.

"All right. My fault," he said, reaching out and gently brushing a strand of hair from her eyes. "I'll be on my best behavior from now on. Word of honor."

His flashing eyes belied his words. "Sure," she said, smiling. "How about Wednesday at ten?"

"Anytime. I'm all yours." He winked.

"Just be here. That's all I ask."

"What about tomorrow? Why are we waiting until Wednesday?"

"Because I have other clients," she answered. "And I need time to work on my plans for you."

He raised a brow. "Sounds interesting. Try to make them elaborate and very, very personal. But what if I think of something important in the meantime? Can I get in touch with you over the weekend or is your home number off-limits too?"

"No, it's not off-limits. Here," she said, taking a card out of her desk drawer. It was one of those she had had specially made up with her office and home phone numbers on it.

"Oh, I bet you give these to all your clients," he said, mocking sadness.

"Yes, I do, as a matter of fact. We'll be working closely together, and —"

He was shaking his head. "You really know how to tear a guy down, don't you?"

"Oh, stop," she said, smiling. "Just go home, relax, and come back on Wednesday."

"How about a quick spin to Easthampton? No strings, no expectations, just a chance to catch up on old times."

"You're impossible!" she cried. "Now, leave before I decide you're too crazy to have as a client."

"Okay. Just one thing though," he said softly, leaning against the desk.

"What's that?"

"Whenever you think about me this weekend — and I know you have to because you said you had to make plans — I'll be thinking about you. Any minute of the day. Or night."

"Get *out* of here!" she cried, pushing him to the door. At first both her hands were against his shoulders. But when he laughed and shifted, she was suddenly pushing against his chest, her fingertips and palms aware of the warm, muscled flesh beneath his shirt. As if with minds of their own, her fingers sought and found his nipples beneath his shirt, and they grew instantly hard under her touch.

"If you really want me to go," he said huskily, "then you shouldn't touch me like that." His voice was like a caress, like a dare to resist . . . and a dare she'd have to lose on. For before she could even think, his warm hands had encircled her waist and brought her closer, and her breasts brushed up against his chest and her nipples tingled with need. His hard lean form insisted against her, and when she realized he was as quickly aroused as she, she knew she had made a mistake getting that close. She had thought of him too many times — she had thought of him too many times to resist. . . .

His lips brushed against hers and closed over her mouth, and he brought his hands up between their bodies, covering her breasts and catching her nipples quickly, expertly, between teasing fingers. She moaned deep into his mouth, warming to his touch, wanting more, when there was a knock at the door.

She tore her mouth away and quickly

wrested herself from his grasp. One deep breath, a glance, and then, "Come in!" she called.

The door opened and her partner, Sloan Hammond, stepped in. He was classically handsome, with graying sideburns and a rich, low voice that always performed miracles over the phone. Andrea had begun dating him when she had first worked for him, and she felt he was one of the few men in the world who would have not only kept her on but actually promoted her when they had broken up after three and a half months. There were still lingering embers of their relationship that occasionally burned bright — if they danced together at a party, if they worked late together at night. But Sloan and Andrea could also work together for days at a time without ever thinking of the past.

Now, though, as Andrea realized her pulling away from Jim had been absolutely frantic, she saw that she had cared a lot about Sloan's not seeing her in Jim's arms. Was that a professional concern, or a more personal one?

"We were just ending our meeting, Sloan," she said after he apologized for interrupting, "but I'm glad you came in. I'd like you to meet Jim Haynes."

"A real pleasure," Sloan said as the two men shook hands. "You played a couple of dozen mean games I was lucky enough to watch."

"And a lot more that weren't so mean you were lucky enough to miss," Jim laughed. "Listen — it was nice meeting you and I'm sure we'll talk again. But you two obviously have things to discuss. So, Andrea, I'll see you Wednesday."

"Right," she said, surprised by his sudden interest in leaving.

A few moments later, as she and Sloan went over the details of a young actress's new contract with Minerva Pictures, Andrea realized Sloan was waiting for her answer to a question she hadn't even heard.

She had been thinking about Jim. . . .

CHAPTER TWO

Jim left the office feeling angry and cheated, and he didn't know why. As he walked up Third Avenue he felt invisible, unrecognized, as if all those years of being cheered on the street had never happened.

He had never been able to understand those Hollywood types who complained on every TV talk show that they had made a big sacrifice when they had gotten famous. Hell, there was nothing better than having a kid give you the thumbs-up and cheer as you passed him on the street. And the women — Lord, he had never dreamed when he was growing up that so many of the fans would be female. And some of them were fanatics — not just women who had been dragged to the game by their husbands.

And then there were the "baseball Annies," the girls who would show up in every city on every tour he had ever taken, ready and willing and eager to make the players happy in every way they knew how.

He had felt great in those early years,

happier than he had ever felt in his life.

And something about the meeting with Andrea made him feel as if it had all turned to mud.

Maybe he had been wrong to come on to her. Maybe he had even offended her. Except that she couldn't have been all that offended to kiss back that way. And kissing her had been the natural thing to do: he was drawn to her immediately. She was damned attractive, with those green eyes and that incredible-looking soft hair. And her body — he had been able to imagine every detail beneath that silk dress — the fullness of her breasts, the curve of her waist, and nipples he'd just love to make hard.

He smiled as he remembered how she had blushed when he had brought up the centerfold. Hell, he hadn't seen a woman blush in years! And the fact she had been blushing because of that picture — it was an exciting idea. To think that she might have been aroused . . .

"Hey! Jim Haynes!" a male voice called.

Jim looked up and saw a man about his own age give a wave.

"They really needed you yesterday out at the stadium!"

Jim smiled. "How about that ninth inning, huh? I would've loved to hear

Jakobson chew out that bastard Cabrini."

"You said it. How's that arm of yours anyway?"

"Okay for everyday life."

The man smiled. "If everyday life is what you're after. Too bad about that. What are you into these days? Real estate? I hear a lot of you guys go into real estate."

"I haven't really decided yet," Jim said, surprising himself. He wondered why the big secret. "Listen, nice talking to you but I've got to go, okay?"

A woman bumped into the man and shot him a glare of pure fury, and the man shrugged, called out "Good luck," and went on his way.

And Jim walked on, feeling that ache of dissatisfaction that he had been feeling before.

That weekend Andrea took the folder of clippings on Jim home, and as she reviewed them, she found that she had forgotten a lot of negative aspects of Jim's personality.

The article accompanying the centerfold was particularly annoying. Andrea was fairly sure that the interview had been hacked and slashed and respliced so that Jim finally sounded like the male chauvinist *Fantasies* seemed to want him to be, but still, how could he have said something like, "I don't think a man is made to be with just one woman — at least 99 percent of the men I know aren't, and that includes me"? Or "I'm surprised a magazine like this can sell; I thought it was just men who were turned on by pictures."

Andrea had laughed but was also irritated. What kind of Stone Age chauvinist was he?

Andrea had grown up in a liberated household, one in which both her mother and father worked, and there had never been any doubt in her mind that she, too, would have a career. It wasn't that she looked down on women who chose family over career; she simply knew what was right for her. And lately she had been thinking — in the back of her mind, anyway — that eventually she'd want to find a balance between her career and the family she hoped to have. She could even visualize quitting her job for a while while her children were young. But if she did this, it certainly wouldn't be because of her husband's wishes. Love or no love, she couldn't imagine doing something like that because of what someone else thought, even if he was her husband. And from the

Fantasies interview, Jim sounded like just the sort of man who would expect her to submit to his wishes in exactly the areas in which she wanted her independence.

Suddenly Andrea caught herself. Why was she thinking about marriage — and Jim? Jim had made a few remarks she didn't like. What she should have been worrying about was changing the image he had inadvertently created. She could teach him how to avoid letting an interviewer twist his words, and she could teach him to say things that wouldn't sound so terrible out of context. She had certainly dealt with less intelligent clients in the past.

But the big question — the one she couldn't answer — was whether Jim was going to let her really help him or not, and whether the relationship would last if he did. For no matter how much power she would seem to have in the coming months — ruling on everything from what he wore to parties to what he said in interviews to what parts he agreed to take — the fact remained that he was the one in real power, and he could fire her if he was unhappy with what she did for him.

She looked down at the article and then at one of the pictures that preceded the centerfold. Jim was smiling out from the magazine, a glint in his dark blue eyes and a smirk on his handsome lips. *Definitely up to something,* she thought. "I love blondes," the caption read, "but I certainly don't rule out anyone else who's pretty, intelligent, and fun."

How wonderfully generous of you! she snarled silently. *What if those blondes, brunettes, and redheads don't want you?*

But the fact was that she did want him despite all the distasteful quotes she had just read. When he had kissed her, something deep inside had given way, had sighed *This is it* with a delicious warmth she had never felt before. And she couldn't forget the feeling.

When she looked at his half-smile that seemed to dare, she remembered the feel of his lips, the warmth of his mouth, the insistent teasing of his tongue. When she looked at his chest and shoulders, so broad and beautifully developed, she remembered the firmness of his chest beneath her fingers, the arousing responsiveness of his hard nipples beneath the smooth cotton shirt. And when she dreamily turned the page and looked at the centerfold picture of Jim, she was mesmerized by the promise of his male form, by the certainty of satisfaction that making love with him would bring. She knew just by looking that he would please her deeply, that he would make her throb with need and then bring her to ecstasy, that his powerful thrusts would be as fiery as his kisses were tender.

You're going to have to make a decision, she told herself as she threw the magazine aside. She was going to have to decide to put Jim Haynes out of her mind as an imaginary lover, or do something about breaking her rule. She couldn't exist in this limbo in which she spent all her time fantasizing about him and so little time actually working; it certainly wasn't helping her or him. She just couldn't seem to get her mind off the possibilities — his lean legs entwined with hers, his rough hands parting her thighs, his hard strength stroking her to blazing passion.

But she couldn't make a decision; the alternative of writing Jim off was just unrealistic, and giving in was too tempting to ever seriously forget about. And then she remembered something she had completely put out of her mind. Jim Haynes, in spite of Andrea giving him the benefit of the doubt concerning his quotes being taken out of context, was not a man to be trusted when it came to man–woman relationships. He was a confirmed bachelor, the type of man who would remain forever unattainable, the kind who wanted to remain forever unattached. He was someone with whom she saw no future, someone she definitely didn't need to get involved with at this point in her life.

And so, ironically enough, she was going to choose to put herself right back into the position she was in in high school: she could fantasize about him all she wanted, but that was as far as she'd let things go.

On Saturday night Andrea went out with Stuart Riverby, a man she had met through Sloan. Stuart was an attorney with the firm that handled all of Hammond/Sutton's legal work — one of the city's leading entertainment-law firms.

The evening was painfully awkward and slow, the kind of hesitant, dry-mouthed date Andrea had thought she had put behind her. Stuart was nice enough, but he was apparently incapable of discussing anything other than business, and when he brought Andrea home, he had the nerve to expect to spend the night with her. Andrea couldn't believe it. Hadn't he noticed how there had been absolutely no chemistry between them? Didn't he care?

When Andrea had said a quick good night and gone back into her room, a thought suddenly flashed through her mind. *Jim would never be that insensitive. He would have known I —*

The phone rang and jolted Andrea out of her thoughts. She glanced at her watch. Almost midnight. Lord, how could the evening have dragged on for so long? And who could be calling at this hour?

Suddenly she realized who it was. Stuart was just unaware and clumsy enough to try again, to call from a nearby bar or phone booth.

She answered unenthusiastically, but her heart leapt when the leathery voice at the other end said, "Andrea?" It was Jim.

"Hi, Jim. What's up? How are you?" she said, trying to sound at least slightly less thrilled than she was. All those fantasies and the tension of the unpleasant evening made her very happy to hear from him.

"Well, not too great," he said, his voice so subdued it was almost inaudible. "I had some bad news tonight and I thought you should know about it. I'm sorry I'm calling so late, too, but I had a date and I just got home to get the message."

"I see," she said, irrationally more disturbed by the fact that he had been on a date than by the prospect of bad news. "What happened?"

"It's Owen. His secretary called me tonight. She and I . . . well, we were pretty close at one time. Anyway, I just spoke to her, and she couldn't tell me much, but what she did tell me was pretty bad. Owen's planning to sue me."

"What? Why?"

"Breach of contract, defamation of character, interference with his right to pursue his gainful employment or some term like that — trying to take away his livelihood, I guess."

"I don't understand," Andrea said, sinking down on the bed. "I thought your parting of the ways with Owen was a mutual thing."

There was a silence, and then Jim sighed. "Well, it was in a way, but that was only because I had gotten Owen so damned mad. I just didn't know how angry he really was. She said he's talking about making it for more than a million dollars — which I don't believe for a minute, but even if he makes it for a tenth of that, Andrea —"

"Believe it," she interrupted. "Really, Jim, believe it. I've heard of suits for more. You've got to realize that the kind of money someone like Owen can make if he succeeds with you is enormous. He was probably planning on building his reputation with you and he failed. Maybe he lost some clients when you quit. And that's lost income for him."

"But I had to quit. He was a stone liar and I wasn't going to deal with him for one more day. I didn't even want to deal with *you* because I thought all managers had to be cheats and liars."

"Well, that isn't really the point right now, is it?" she said quietly. "We have to find out if what Owen's secretary said is true and then we have to get ready for it."

"I just can't deal with that kind of vengeance," Jim said. "A million dollars because I left him? Hell, even alimony doesn't get you that much. And if he thought I was worth that much, why didn't he treat me better? If he hadn't lied so much, maybe I'd have stayed."

Andrea could hear the panic in Jim's voice, probably something even he himself didn't recognize. He had always been afraid to show his emotions, and he probably thought it was wrong to admit he was scared. "Look," she said quietly, "the best thing we can do is meet with Sloan and our attorney and see what has to be done.

They both have more experience in this than I do, and believe me when I tell you their experiences have been good, not bad. Now, I can probably get Sloan to meet with us Monday morning. If what Owen's secretary said is true, there's going to be a lot of immediate and negative publicity about you getting cranked out by Owen's team. But maybe we should meet tomorrow. I'm going to have to know everything you can think of that Owen might say."

"What about your lawyer? Wouldn't I just tell it to him?"

"At two hundred fifty dollars an hour, no, Jim. I'd rather hear it from you and get it down to essentials."

"Okay, hold on a second."

He covered the mouthpiece before she could even say okay, and Andrea realized for the first time — though she knew she should have thought of it before — that Jim's date was still at his apartment. And the knowledge gnawed at her. When he had first called, after all, she had assumed it was for personal reasons — probably because of the constant fantasizing she had been doing. She had been disappointed he had called only for business reasons, and now that she knew he had another woman at his apartment, she was brought back to reality with a cold rush of disappointment. What had she been thinking of for the past few days? She had let her mind and imagination wander way too far. The reality was that Jim had a whole life she didn't know anything about; she was a small part of his life — that was all. And she'd have to remember that.

"Andrea? What time were you thinking of?"

"Oh, the afternoon would be good enough. Just so we're able to go over enough to present Sloan with on Monday morning. As I said, he does have more experience with this than I do."

Jim was sure he heard a new coldness in Andrea's voice. When had it started? She sounded all business now, as if he had hurt her in some way. But wasn't she the one who had said that that was the way she wanted it?

He looked over at Claudia, who was pacing in front of the terrace doors. She was beautiful — blond, sleek, the kind of woman he had wanted from the minute he had been interested in girls.

He had planned to spend the whole weekend with her, and now Andrea wanted to see him tomorrow. But she wanted to see him because of the Owen thing.

"Jim? What's the story? Can you make it or not?" Andrea said impatiently.

"What? Oh, yeah. Sure. Of course," he said, realizing he had no choice. Hell, it was his career — and maybe his financial security — on the line. "Any time you say, Andrea."

"Okay, say two o'clock then, at my office."

"Your office?"

"Yes. I'll see you then," she said quickly, and added, "and bring your contract with Owen" before she hung up.

Jim shook his head. Suddenly he didn't want to be with Claudia and he didn't want to even think about being with Andrea. They were both totally impossible to understand. Andrea had told him she wasn't interested in a personal relationship. But he could swear she had cooled when she found out why he had called. And Claudia — he just didn't want to be with her.

He turned to her, but she was looking out the window, standing motionless with a glass of white wine in her hand.

"Claud?"

She turned. She looked upset, her pale blue eyes misty. "Why didn't you tell *me* about all that Owen business?" she cried. "I have ears, too, you know."

He stared. "Claudia, we just got home ten minutes ago and I listened to the tape *nine* minutes ago."

For a moment she was silent, biting her lip and looking down into her wine. Then she raised her eyes to his. "Still," she said quietly, "I thought we had agreed you'd talk to me more. About *everything*, Jim — *everything*."

"This is *not* the time to start an argument," he said quietly. "I'm not really in the mood to talk about anything, but if I were, it wouldn't be what we have or haven't agreed to."

She looked alarmed. "What does that mean? I thought you said we were going to tell each other when things bothered us. You agreed."

"Look. Don't you understand? I'm not in the mood to talk, all right? I've just had some bad news and I want to be alone."

"Jim, come on! You told me we were going to spend the whole weekend together!"

"The plan has changed, all right?"

Claudia took a sip of wine and then looked at him. "So you want me to leave now?"

He sighed and stepped forward and took her in his arms. "It's not you, okay? But I have to do some thinking tonight for my meeting with Andrea tomorrow, and I have to be alone."

"Well, okay," she said quietly. "As long as it's not me."

He shook his head. "I promise you it's not," he said softly. He knew that his words were only half true, but he didn't want to hurt her.

A few minutes later, after she was gone, he wished he had been less harsh when they parted. There was no need to hurt her; he had just wanted to be alone. He had to think about Owen and the lawsuit and all the bitterness and arguments and lies that had led up to it, and Claudia was not the intelligent and sympathetic company he needed.

All he could think about was Andrea. He remembered those incredible warm lips of hers, her moan from deep inside as he thrust his tongue into her mouth, the pounding of her heart as his chest pressed against her breasts. He remembered the feel of her taut nipples beneath her blouse as he raked them with his fingers, the urgency of his own male response as he brought her close. And he knew he had to have more of her, that they were meant for each other. There were other women — beautiful women — who perhaps matched Andrea in looks. But their responses — and his own — were nothing compared to those that had occurred when he was with Andrea. And he could just imagine gently exploring every inch of her, running his lips along thighs he knew would be like warm silk, parting her lips with his tongue and making her surge and cry out with pleasure. And suddenly thought wasn't enough. He was so aroused. . . .

And he knew he'd do whatever he had to in order to make her his.

The next day, as Andrea sat next to Jim on her office couch, she felt he wasn't really concentrating.

"Do you understand what I'm saying?" she asked. "This lawsuit — Owen needed you before. He probably told every prospective client that he was Jim Haynes's personal manager. You're famous enough that that was really impressive, because those prospective clients didn't know that Owen was creating an image you didn't want. All they cared about was that you were famous, and they wanted to be too. And now you've taken what was essentially a very powerful marketing tool out of Owen's hands. Which means he's going to fight very hard to make it seem as if you were at fault."

He shook his head. "I was really willing to forget," he said. "I was willing to forget all his mistakes and lies and fake deals and interviews. But now . . ." He sighed. "Do you know that he actually told me he had the president of Aries Pictures panting to sign me up for a picture and that I had carte blanche to bring him a 'picture of my choice,' as he put it? That's fraud, isn't it?"

"Of course it is," she said, reaching for a pad. She scratched out a few notes and then looked at Jim. "And that's exactly the kind of thing I need to know. Specific instances, Jim. Our lawyer will want to know the exact dates if you can remember them, but give me what you can now."

Jim shook his head. "There's just so much. He was really getting paranoid at the end, for one thing. He had told so many lies — and he knew it — that he couldn't keep track of what they were and what he had said to whom. He had this big-deal office on Park Avenue — at Fifty-ninth Street — which I don't even think he was paying for at the end, because I heard him talking to the landlord when I was there and he'd tell people his secretaries were out, that his teams of assistants were out, and he had only one woman, probably his mother, working for him the whole time. But that office was magnificent — a suite of rooms with French antiques, and I think they were all real — tables, chairs, chaise longues — everything. Anyway, I see what you meant about using me to sell other people on the idea of Fielding Creative Management, because what sold me was the atmosphere. I figured he couldn't be a ripoff artist if he had that beautiful office; he had to be a success. But anyway — his lies. I'd sit in his office — and he had this way of making you sit there for hours, and if you'd try to leave, he'd say you were too temperamental and irresponsible. But because I was there so much, I heard a lot of his conversations. I'd hear him tell one client — all I know about her is that she was an actress and her name was Deirdre. I heard him tell her that she was one of two actresses being considered for a part on that new soap opera that started last month. Then I heard him tell the same damn thing — in the same words — to three other women. By the end of the afternoon I must have been staring at him or looking angry, because he shrugged and said something like, 'Oh, don't give what you just heard another thought. It's all part of the business and it keeps their confidence up.' "

Andrea shook her head. "It's not part of *my* business."

Jim was fired up now and hardly aware that she had even spoken. "Oh, and there was the time Owen presented me with what he called an easy choice. I supposedly had a 'fantastic' chance at a small and short-lived part on a soap where he was supposedly very close with the producer. Or I could do a beer commercial, something that my soap contract would have ruled out because they didn't want their actors doing endorsements. The beer commercial was actually something that had nothing to do with Owen. I had been approached directly because of baseball — they didn't even know I wanted to become an actor. Anyway, Owen was sure I was going to go for the beer commercial because it was going to pay a hell of a lot more for a hell of a lot longer than this little nothing part on the soap. So he built up the soap part to make himself look like the great Owen Fielding who could do anything for his clients. He was supposedly presenting me with a very difficult choice. But he was sure I was going to go for the beer commercial. And then I told him I wanted the soap part."

"You're kidding! Did you know you were calling his bluff?"

"Oh, maybe I half-knew. I think I suspected, at that point, that he was taking me for a ride, but I didn't want to believe it. And then I tested it."

"So what did he do?"

"He had no choice," Jim said, smiling. "He had to send me to the audition, and when I didn't get the part, he just said it was a fluke — even though he had pretty much promised it was mine. It was one of the hundreds of incidents I can look back on now and say, I should have known. But I didn't want to know, so I didn't. It just taught me not to put myself in someone's hands like that."

"But you have," she said. "You've put yourself in *my* hands, Jim, in exactly the same role Owen had. And I really don't think you're comfortable with that."

He smiled, his dark blue eyes velvety as they looked into hers. "Will you let me worry about that, please? It's completely different and you know it."

"I don't know it," she said spiritedly.

"And I think you should think about it before you let your resentment for what I'm doing build up."

He shook his head slowly. "The last thing I feel for you is resentment, Andrea. I promise you that." He reached out and cupped her cheek in a warm hand, then ran his hand down her neck and edged it beneath the fabric of her blouse. The touch of his rough fingers against her smooth skin was warm, suggestive, seductive. She wanted to tell him to stop, but more than that, she wanted him to go on. She hadn't forgotten his kisses, his touch, the pleasure he could give. . . .

"Something happened to me last night," he said softly, capturing her gaze in his. "I don't know what set me off, but I think it had to do with the fact that I was with someone else when I called you. And I wished I were with you, Andrea."

She said nothing for a moment, melting beneath his touch as his other hand began tracing lazy circles around her knee and along her lower thigh. "Jim, I —"

"Just tell me," he whispered.

"Tell you what?"

"Tell me you didn't think about me just once this weekend."

She smiled. "Of course I thought of you.

I told you I'd be making plans."

"That's not what I'm talking about," he murmured huskily, his warm hand moving up the soft skin of her thigh. A burning glow began to grow deep inside her, muddling her thoughts and making her voice thick with need as she said, "Jim, don't."

"I won't if you don't want me to," he whispered. He brought his face close then, his lips brushing against hers, gently and silently telling her how much pleasure they could give her if only she would let him. She knew how he'd run his warm, wet tongue along her inner thighs, how he'd tease her with his lips and the tip of his tongue, how his scratchy cheeks would make her soft skin tingle. "Tell me you want me to stop," he murmured. She thought of his hard thighs parting hers with a force she'd welcome, of the cries of pleasure he'd make her shout, of the breathless ecstasy that would be theirs if only she said yes. "Tell me," he whispered.

She looked up into his eyes — beautiful deep blue, dark with desire, hypnotic.

"Don't stop," she said hoarsely, and with a moan he brought his lips to hers, entering her mouth with his warm tongue as he laid her back on the sofa.

His hard frame parted her thighs as he

lay on top of her, and she arched with need as his warm hand began to work its way upward, and she craved his touch more and more desperately.

Suddenly Jim realized he was making a mistake — a big mistake. Andrea was a strong woman. She knew what she wanted; that was one of the reasons he wanted her. But right now she was uncertain. Sure, she was responsive — he hadn't been kissed like this in a long time. But later on how would she feel? Probably as if he were rushing her, as if he had pushed her into the embrace. And there was only one thing to do when you were feeling pushed: push back. And he didn't want her to do that.

He wanted her to dream of him, to want him as she ate and slept and worked; he wanted her to think she saw him on the street and then realize she had only been hoping . . . but it wasn't him. He wanted her to wish that every phone call was from him, that every letter was about him. He wanted her to ache for him, to dream of him, to be possessed by fantasies of making love until dawn every night. And when he finally came to her, he'd rock her to the core, fill her with more love than she had ever had in her life.

"We have to stop," he whispered into the

scented sweetness of her neck.

Her green eyes were dark with desire. "Why?" she murmured thickly. She could hardly speak; she felt as if she had been drawn into a dream, as if none of her thinking and reasoning and rationality made a bit of sense anymore. What was important — more than anything else — was that she had never been reached like this so quickly, that she wanted him more than she had ever wanted anyone in her life.

He drew her up so she was looking into his beautiful eyes, and she felt as if she were drowning in their azure depths.

"For one thing, Andrea, I don't think you're really the type to enjoy making love at the office — for the first time, anyway. Even *I* think it's tacky and there's almost nothing on earth that's tacky to me."

She laughed.

"For another thing, I think maybe we should slow down."

She smiled. "That's the part I'm not so sure I agree with."

"Well, that's just too bad. We *do* have work to do, you know."

She reached out and traced a finger along his lips. "You are a manipulating and transparent game-player, and you might just find that this little scheme of yours is going to backfire!"

He raised a dark brow. "Is that so?"

"*I* think so," she said confidently. But deep inside she was wondering what he actually felt for her. When he had first drawn back, she thought he was just playing games, that he was trying to show her how much she really did want him. But then a new thought struck her, and it hurt: what if the game were serious, and not really a game at all? What if he really wasn't interested, and was stringing her along because he thought it would help his career? Now that she really liked him and was ready to throw away the rulebook, perhaps the game had changed.

CHAPTER THREE

"Let's see. I have it here somewhere," Andrea said.

Sloan Hammond watched as his beautiful young partner looked through her folder, and he knew something was wrong. She was distracted, confused, unsure of what she was saying.

"You know," she said abstractedly as she continued to look through her notes, "this Owen Fielding actually told Jim not to try out for the Dick Goudreau part in that new Jared Roberts play?"

"You told me that," Sloan said. "Now, why don't you tell me what's bothering you."

"What?" Andrea looked up, but her eyes didn't meet Sloan's.

"Something's bothering you," Sloan said gently. "Why don't you tell me what it is?"

Andrea shrugged. "Oh. Really. It's nothing," she said weakly.

Sloan leaned back in his chair and relit his pipe. "Now, come on," he chided. "We go back way too far for this."

As he puffed on his pipe the sweet smell of his tobacco brought Andrea back to the time when Sloan had first hired her. She had been ridiculously overconfident back then, twenty-four years old, with nothing but a college education and two years of secretarial work at a public relations agency behind her. She had told him she could turn his agency around, which was absurd because she was so green and even more absurd because he was doing quite well without her. But he had hired her, and she had fallen for him very slowly, very gradually, during long evenings when they were both working late, during early-morning breakfast meetings when they tackled the most difficult problems. She had loved his confidence, his self-assuredness, his strength; she had loved the way he was so unselfconscious about his good looks, and she had loved his success; and most of all she had loved his honesty and his gentleness.

Yet they hadn't been able to sustain the relationship. He shared fewer and fewer of his good qualities with her as time went on; he wasn't the perfect man she had thought he was. And there were other difficulties. Andrea discovered that what she thought was love was a crush, a very strong crush that had conveniently made her love her job. Sloan was fifteen years older than she was, and there were many things she wanted out of life that he didn't want anymore. Children, for one thing. He had had two, gotten divorced, and was sure he never wanted to marry again. But that wasn't even an issue, because one day Andrea woke up and knew she wanted the relationship to end. They had gone as far as they could.

Somehow — and Andrea would never have thought this was possible — they managed to continue to work together. And they were better friends than they had ever been in the three and a half months they had gone out together.

Yet now she felt uncomfortable under Sloan's scrutiny. "I'd really rather not talk about it," she said as gently as she could.

He shrugged. "Okay. But if you want an ear, or a shoulder to cry on, I'm here."

She smiled. "Thanks. I know. And it isn't crying material, thank God."

"Good. So tell me what else we've got."

"All right. Let's see. Here's what I was looking for. . . ." She started to tell him about another lie Owen had told Jim — this one about a supposed poster offer he was weighing. As she spoke, Andrea seemed almost consumed by the injustice of what Owen had done. She became so angry that dark blotches of red appeared on her cheeks. "What I find so amazing about all of this is that half the time Owen didn't even get anything out of the lies he told Jim and his other clients! He didn't get any extra money by steering them to a particular arrangement or job, and it just infuriates me that the lies were so pervasive and that in a lot of cases they didn't even have a point!"

"But that's where you're wrong," Sloan said. "He wanted to make himself seem as powerful as he could to his clients. He didn't have to make money directly from each lie; he was creating an image for himself — of the great Owen Fielding. After that was in place, then he could start counting the money."

"But, damn it, how did he expect to make money if he was such a fraud? I mean, even if his clients didn't know he was a liar, he certainly had to know. So once he had these clients he lied to get, how was he going to make money from them?"

"Oh, he had enough going for him legitimately, Andrea. I remember when he started in the business — a little before my own time, but I was following it. He had some pretty big names. And he has a brother who runs a very legitimate and respected theater in Boston — which isn't the key to fame and success, but it certainly doesn't hurt."

Andrea shook her head. "It just makes me so furious! Someone like Jim who has so much talent. And all the others. . . ."

"I think the 'others' wouldn't be of that much concern to you if it weren't for Jim," he said quietly.

She looked up into Sloan's dark brown eyes. "What do you mean?"

He sighed. "Andrea, I don't want to venture where I'm not wanted, but we go back too far for me not to say anything. You and Jim: I wish you'd give it some thought." He smiled. "And don't look so surprised, kid. You've always worn your heart on your sleeve."

"Is it that obvious?"

"Probably only to your friends." He laughed. "All your friends, that is."

But she didn't smile. "I really don't know what's happening to me, Sloan. Jim Haynes walked in here just a few days ago, and I really can't think of anything or anyone else."

Sloan hurt when he heard those words.

Lovely Andrea. He wanted her to be happy; and he knew things could never work between them. She deserved too much that he couldn't give her. He did want her to be happy, but when he heard her say she couldn't think of anything else, it hurt.

He relit his pipe and leaned back in his chair. "Look," he said softly. "My feelings about this are a little complicated. I like Jim Haynes — I liked him as a ballplayer and he seems like a nice enough guy. And you know how I feel about . . . how I feel about you. But you also know how dangerous it is to get involved with a client, Andrea. Nine times out of ten everything goes sour, including the professional relationship."

"That didn't happen with Sylvia Masters. You still have *her* as a client."

He shrugged. "Okay, so she's the one time in ten. You know what I'm saying, Andrea."

She sighed and shook her head. "I just wish I knew what the situation really was. One moment I think he really likes me, but then the next . . . Yesterday I began to wonder whether he was doing what he was doing because it would help his career."

"You don't really trust him then?"

"I do trust him," she said quickly. "Just not — not in terms of the relationship. And I know he has at least one other girlfriend."

"Andrea —"

"I *know* how bad that sounds, Sloan. I can tell myself that there are about a hundred strikes against the idea of my going out with him. I can tell myself that I kind of made a deal with myself last year that I wasn't going to go out with anyone who didn't have a lot of potential in every way. If I read about Jim Haynes in an advice to the lovelorn column, I'd say, Stay away from him, honey. He's bad news. But I can't stop thinking about him."

At first Sloan said nothing. He recognized the situation, and there really was nothing to say. He had felt as helpless as Andrea once with Andrea herself, when he had told himself to stay away from her because she was his assistant, because the end would almost certainly be very unhappy. And he remembered how those cautionary and usually wise words hadn't made a dent in his feelings.

"I just don't want to see you hurt," he finally said, his voice heavy with emotion.

She smiled. "I know. And I appreciate it."

And when Jim came a half-hour later to talk to them both, Andrea thought it was sweet the way Sloan was studying Jim, looking for flaws and good points in a way that was obvious to her but had probably escaped Jim's notice entirely.

"Isn't there a way we can find out today whether Fielding is going to go ahead or not?" Sloan asked.

Jim shrugged. "Jill said she'd let me know the minute she heard more. She told me all she knows."

"And you're sure you can trust her?" Sloan asked.

"Absolutely."

Sloan glanced at Andrea, and she smiled inwardly. Talk about getting distracted by emotions! Sloan now seemed more interested in evaluating Jim as Andrea's prospective boyfriend than in the case.

"All right," Sloan said, folding his hands. "I certainly have enough to give our lawyer for now. His name is Charles Danforth. He may want this Jill's home number, Jim, but in the meantime I think we should just sit tight. And you agree not to talk to your lawyer about this."

Jim nodded. "Sure. How can I? He was Owen's lawyer and I'm sure he's handling this case. That was another rule of Owen's, by the way: all his clients had to retain his lawyer as theirs."

Sloan shook his head. "Mighty convenient. Well, I'm sure this guy will know why you haven't contacted him, but we can't help that. Of course, you're using our lawyer now, too, but I want you to get your own after this case. Danforth's a specialist, though, so I really think he's your best bet. Anyway, I know Andrea has some pretty good news for you, so I'll leave you two alone for now."

Sloan picked up his papers and left the room, and Andrea smiled inwardly: he really was sweet.

And then Jim said, "So tell me the news!"

She smiled. "All right. Don't get *too* excited, because I'm not Owen and I'm not going to lie to you. You don't have this part. But the producers of this film know you and loved the idea of casting you in this role, and Sloan did a good job of talking you up, so —"

"Sloan?" Jim interrupted. "Why not you?"

"Oh, he knows them better and they called him, and we both do what we can for our clients. There are really no rigid divisions in this office. Anyway, it's a very small part, but it's —"

"How small?" he cut in.

"I'll *tell* you if you let me finish. Don't you even want to know what the film is or who the producers are, or who's in it?"

"Okay, *tell* me what the film is and who the producers are and who's in it. And then tell me about my part."

"Okay. It sounds really great. It's being produced by Alexander and Eva Kropotkin, the team that did *Morning Splendor* and *Paley's Revenge*. Both, you probably know, were huge box-office successes *and* Academy Award–winners. *Revenge* got seven nominations and won two awards. The movie is probably going to be called *The Princess of Destiny*, and it'll be about a woman who's both used and a user, the wife of a world-famous trial lawyer and how she unwittingly gets involved in an international espionage ring. So far Jake Curtis is going to be the male lead, which right there guarantees the movie will be a giant hit, and Lynda Palmer is ninety-nine percent set to play the female lead. You, Jim Haynes, former first baseman of the New York Aces and future star, might, if everything goes right, play Lynda Palmer's lover, a character named Kyle Whiting."

"You're kidding."

She smiled. "Nope. Don't get too excited though. You have to try out just like anybody else who's starting out. But you do have a big edge because, as I said, they did love the idea."

"That's fantastic! So what do we do? When do I start learning my lines? When can I go see them?"

She laughed. "Gee, it's too bad you're not excited about this, Jim, because I had had such high hopes."

"Andrea, come on."

"Okay. First of all, there aren't that many lines. It's a *significant* part, but as I said, it's very small. So I wouldn't worry too much about learning the lines. I mean don't get nervous about that."

"How small?" he asked quietly.

"Well, actually, it's one scene, and I'd say you have fifteen lines."

"Fifteen?"

"Fifteen or twenty. Certainly no more than that."

"Are you kidding? Andrea, I can't believe you made this big a deal out of a part that has fewer than twenty lines!"

"Jim, it's a fantastic part!"

"Come on! If it's so fantastic, why is it so

small? I can't believe — Look, if Sloan is such a great friend of the producers, why can't he get them to make it bigger? Just a little rewriting to make it a little bigger. If they really want me in the part, they'll probably do it." He blinked. "What's the matter?"

"I can't believe what I'm hearing, that's all. Five minutes ago you were someone who was just starting out. And not only that, you were someone who's just come out of a pretty bad experience with a pretty bad and very dishonest manager. You're starting ahead of a lot of people, Jim, because of who you are, but *you're* the one — not me — you're the one who said you wanted quality parts and didn't want to be thought of as beefcake for the rest of your career. And now —"

"That's all true," he cut in. "But that doesn't mean I have to grab the first crappy part that comes along."

She rolled her eyes. "I don't believe it! Crappy? There *is* no such thing as a crappy part in an Alexander and Eva Kropotkin movie. Especially in a movie starring Jake Curtis and probably Lynda Palmer. Or if not her, someone equally famous. Jim, you are just starting out. How many times do I have to tell you that?"

"You don't have to tell me again," he

said. "I know what you think." He paused, his clear blue eyes sparkling brightly. "Just tell me one thing. Are you saying this is the best you can do?"

That was too much. "It's not the best I could do for Jack Shaw or Steve Baxter, who are both my clients. And I could do better for Pete Turner and Rick Danvers, who are also my clients. And for half a dozen other clients of mine who have more experience — much more experience — than you do. It is the best I can do for you now, Jim. One of the other things I was going to tell you today was that I spoke with Olga Rafelson this morning, and she's willing to have you audition this week for her classes, private *and* group, and very hard to get into. I've seen her work miracles with clients, Jim. And if she does with you, then fine, we can talk about bigger parts. But right now, you're really lucky — damned lucky — to get the chance to try out for the Kropotkin movie."

He sat there shaking his head and saying nothing, which infuriated her. What she had said was something he had to have known anyway.

Finally he leveled his blue eyes at her and said, "I should have known," so quietly she barely heard him.

"Should have known what?" she snapped.

He sighed. "I should have known that you're all alike in the end."

"What are you talking about?"

He shook his head again. "It was the exact same way with Owen. When I first spoke with him, the first two or three times, he acted as if he could turn me into a star overnight. Everything was going to be wonderful, I was going to be getting million-dollar contracts, the works. That was to get me to sign with him. And then the honeymoon was over damned quickly. All of a sudden my demands were 'unreasonable' and 'irrational.' He worked and worked and worked until he had my confidence so low that I thought anything he could do for me — no matter how small — was a miracle."

"Jim, I really —"

"No, listen to me," he said forcefully. "I just had a long talk with my little sister — I don't know if you remember her — Katie. Or Kate now, actually."

Andrea shook her head.

"Well, I guess you wouldn't, because she's twelve years younger than I am. But anyway, she decided she didn't want to go to college right away. She went to see our cousins in California this summer, and now that it's September, she was planning on getting a job in the city. Now, Katie is a really good kid; she's not spoiled, she's not a snob, she's just a great kid and she's not the biggest intellectual in the world. She just wants a job in a field where she can make something of herself even though she doesn't have a college degree. And do you know something? I spent all Friday night trying to get that kid to stop crying because of what some bitch down at an employment agency told her. Do you want to know what that — that woman told her? That she'd be lucky to get *any* job with so little experience, and that she'd probably, quote, never get anywhere, unquote, because her typing isn't all that great. And this same woman — this exact same woman — told her two weeks before, when she first walked in, that she'd get her a job in fashion or cosmetics, whichever she preferred, for a starting salary of two-fifty a week. Now, how do you explain that?"

Andrea sighed. "Look, Jim, I'm sorry about your sister and what happened to her. Really. But for you to compare what happened to her with what I just told you —"

"It's the same damned thing!" he cried. "Lure them in with promises, knock down their confidence to the point where they'll take anything, then stick them with a job no one else wants."

"And is that what you think I'm doing?"

"I'm not happy so far," he said hoarsely. "That's all I know. And if you think about some of the things you've said to me, Andrea, you'll see exactly what I'm talking about. It has nothing to do with you as Andrea. I've always liked you and I always will. But, damn it, until today we were *not* talking about fifteen-line parts." He stood up. "When you've come up with something better, you can call me," he said, and he strode to the door, yanked it open, and left before she could say another word.

Andrea stood up from the conference table and swore under her breath. That kind of outburst happened with nearly every client at some point; they began thinking they were bigger than life and suddenly nothing was good enough for them. But how could it happen to Jim so quickly? He was just starting out.

Then she realized that the terrible and rocky relationship he had had with Owen had taught him to trust no one in

Andrea's role. He had just been getting used to the idea of having hired her when Owen slapped an enormous lawsuit on him — or was about to. And his sister, Katie, just to make things worse, had had an awful experience with an agency.

And to top it all off, Andrea had led him to believe he was about to audition for what he probably thought was the world's greatest part. And when he heard how small it was, he just cracked.

She could see how it had happened; she had seen the look of hurt in his eyes, that look of shocked surprise that explained it all. And she did understand why he felt as he did. He was already famous; he had already had the kind of career most people only dream of. Getting there had been difficult, but he had done it. And now the second career he wanted so badly wasn't coming as easily as he had expected it to and he felt cheated.

And Andrea understood. But she couldn't let him wallow in his feelings. She had seen actors and actresses buried by the exact same feelings, so consumed by mistrust, self-righteousness, fear, and deep uncertainty that they had never been able to get up and fight again. They said they believed in themselves, but all they really wanted or cared about was what other people thought, and they grew to believe no one was on their side. And they sought solace in drugs, drinking, and self-pity.

She didn't think Jim was self-destructive though. He had just had a lot happen to him, and it was happening too quickly.

She had to make him see she was on his side — that she was, that Sloan was, that they were a team and that he had to play as part of a team just as he had been part of the Aces.

And she had to make him read for the role in *The Princess of Destiny*. She knew — even if he didn't — that the part was perfect for him in every way. It would give him maximum exposure with minimum risk in a film that was quality yet commercial at the same time. And, too, there was the matter of Andrea and Sloan's answer to the producers. Sloan had already told Eva Kropotkin that Jim would audition next week, having assumed, as Andrea had, that he'd be thrilled. Now it would look strange or worse for Andrea to call back and say Jim wouldn't be trying out after all. It just didn't make a bit of sense to alienate Eva and Alexander Kropotkin.

And the most frustrating part of all was

that Jim had a damned good chance of getting the part if he tried out for it. Sloan had told Andrea that Eva had laughed her famous throaty laugh when Sloan had mentioned Jim as a possibility. She had sent the script over by messenger, and the clear understanding was that unless Jim was absolutely atrocious, he'd get the part.

Andrea yanked the script off a pile of other scripts on her desk, and hurried to wrap up the rest of her day's business. She rushed through five calls in a row, and after hurriedly ending a sixth, it occurred to her that she was bending way over backward in Jim's favor. If any other client had said what Jim had said to her, she would have insisted on a serious rethinking period — on both sides — before resuming business, whereas with Jim, she was sending off a script to his house as if nothing had ever happened.

But she felt it was her only choice. If Eva or Alexander called tomorrow, she could hardly say, Well, I'm not sure Jim will read the script because we're mad at each other. She had to give it another try. And she'd deal later on with what he had said to her.

She wrote a short note to Jim and attached it to the script:

> I *urge* you to read this, Jim. You will really see what a good part it is. And even if you don't like it, call my office tomorrow morning. Rachelle will make arrangements to get the script back. *Do this no matter what!*
>
> Andrea.

While she was angrily shoving the script and note into an envelope, Sloan came in.

"Hey! Hey!" he cried out. "That isn't garbage, Andrea. Slow down!"

"It won't fit into the damned envelope!"

"Then try another size," he said, calmly extricating the nearly mangled script from the now torn envelope. "Here. Give me another. And don't look so angry. You've come into my office a thousand times and seen me do the same thing. Just tell me one thing: Is it Jim you wish you were shoving into an envelope like that?"

She laughed. It sounded ridiculous, but it was true. "Well, yes, damn it," she said. And she told him about the fight she and Jim had had.

He shook his head and sat down on her

desk. "You do see what the problem is, don't you?"

"Yes! He's being a jerk about the script and about you and about me!"

"He's reacting the way a lot of clients do at some point. Don't think it has that much to do with you, Andrea. Remember the lawsuit and what he's just come through with Owen."

She sighed. "I know. I told myself the same thing. But I'm just wondering why I'm going out of my way to — I don't know . . ." Her voice trailed off.

"Because he's a client. You want him to read that script, don't you? Fight or no fight?"

"I just wish —"

He shook his head. "Just set up a professional relationship that works. The rest will either come or not come."

She sighed. "I guess you're right."

Sloan nodded. But he felt like anything but a good friend at the moment. He was jealous of Jim Haynes. The guy had everything going for him — great looks, one successful career already behind him, certainly more money than most people ever imagined making. And he had Andrea dreaming of him. He could see it in her eyes; he had seen it when they were all together discussing Jim's plans — the way Jim would look at her and she seemed to bloom under his gaze, the way a mildly funny comment of Jim's made her laugh with pleasure. And now he saw something in Andrea's eyes that she probably didn't even know was there — fear. Fear that she had lost Jim before she had ever had him, fear that the whole relationship had already collapsed. And, damn it, he couldn't help hoping it *wouldn't* work out.

It wasn't even that he wanted Andrea for himself anymore. But he didn't want to see her with someone else if it had to happen in front of his very eyes. He didn't want to think about the passion that burned inside of her being spent for someone else. And he could see in her eyes that she was already caught.

"Where does this Haynes live?" he suddenly asked.

"First and Seventy-fifth. Right near me actually."

"And you're going to drop the script off in person?"

"I'm going to leave it with the doorman," she said. "Why?"

"Well, I'm going that way myself, and —"

She smiled. "You're not jealous?"

"I don't want to see you get hurt."

Andrea looked into his eyes. "I'm not going to," she said quietly. "Especially because the more you say that, Sloan, the more I realize I'm strong enough to take care of myself."

"I hope so."

"I am," she said firmly and with a bit of annoyance. She hated it when Sloan was so negative.

And a few minutes later, as she left with the newly wrapped script in tow, she realized that in a sense Sloan's cautionary warnings — which she suspected weren't completely good-willed — *did* make her feel stronger. She knew what she was about even if she didn't always act that way.

The moment Jim had gotten home the phone rang, and he let the answering machine pick it up as he tore off his sweat-drenched shirt. The call was from Andrea, he was willing to bet. And, damn it, he didn't want to talk to her.

He reached over to the machine, though, and turned up the volume: "Jim? This is Claudia. I was wondering how you were feeling today and if —"

He picked up the phone. "Claudia?"

"You're there!"

"Yeah, I just walked in the door."

"Um, how are you? Did you settle anything about that Owen business? You don't have to tell me, but it sounded so awful."

"Nah. Nothing's settled yet. We met, but that's about it."

"Well, how about if I come over? You sound like you could use some cheering up."

"I —"

"Or we could go out," she said quickly and hopefully. "For a drink or dinner or something."

He felt like an incredible heel. He had kicked her out two nights ago and never called her back when she left messages on his machine, and now he was acting as if she were asking him to do some sort of chore.

"Do you want to meet me over at Jason's?" he asked. "We could grab a bite if you're hungry."

"Well, I'm not hungry but I'd like to see you. I can be there in ten minutes, okay?"

"Make it fifteen and you're on. If I don't take a shower I'll drive everyone at Jason's out in about three minutes."

She laughed. "I'll meet you outside or at the bar, Jim. I'm glad we're getting together." Then she hung up.

Forty minutes later Jim was still waiting

for Claudia and getting angrier by the second both at her and himself. He knew Claudia: she liked to make an entrance even if it was only to a grocery store, and he should have known she'd wait until she was sure he'd be there. But had he agreed to come only because he had felt cooped up and angry the moment he had gotten inside his apartment? He had tried to convince himself he was making up for the other night by being nice to Claudia, but what the hell kind of favor was that when he really didn't want to be with her? It wasn't fair to her.

It was the Andrea business that had mixed him all up. He had flown off the handle with her, he didn't know whether he trusted her or not, and now it was all a mess.

As he looked up from his drink at his outdoor table Claudia waved from down the sidewalk and flashed him a big smile, and he felt more like a heel than ever.

Jim's building, a few blocks north of Andrea's, was a modern high rise on the corner, a luxury building known for its excellent security and its large concentration of well-known tenants, most of them sports figures. Clyde Fouquet, the star hockey player with scores of equally famous model-girlfriends, lived there, and Ralph Masterson, the quarterback who had just signed a multimillion-dollar contract with the New York Rockets, lived in a penthouse in the building, as did at least a dozen other famous people who had enough money to pay what had to be outrageous rents for what Andrea skeptically guessed were very small apartments. From the look of the building from the outside, it was about like hers — a sterile-looking near-skyscraper with a "luxury" lobby she could see from the sidewalk because of its huge plate-glass windows, and, she guessed, walls upstairs that were as thin as paper.

The architecture of buildings like Jim's and hers always reminded Andrea of the business she was in: image was more important than substance. Just as in Hollywood, stars and would-be stars gave parties they couldn't afford, bought cars they couldn't pay for, and sometimes even lived in palatial homes that were virtually empty on the inside — all to create the illusion of great success — the architects of Jim's and Andrea's buildings had spared no expense in what the public could see. Jim's lobby was vast and dripping with luxury, with magnificent modern chandeliers that looked like cascades of crystal tears, floor-lit fountains bathed in an almost unearthly white light, exotic plants bursting with flowers whose colors Andrea had never seen before. The doormen — and there were two that Andrea could see — were dressed in a fine navy wool so dark it was almost black, and when she handed Jim's script to one of the men, he said, "He'll get it the moment he gets in, madam," with a thick English accent.

Andrea left the building and headed for her own, thinking about Sloan and how he had acted so strangely about the package. Would he really have delivered it himself just to keep her from what he must have imagined was Jim's apartment rather than just his lobby? Was he really jealous?

There was something unsettling in the thought, because she had always trusted Sloan implicitly — in everything — and now she felt his intentions had been selfish.

It was odd, too, that she felt this way. She had been on the losing end in so many relationships that she had always felt it would be wonderful and glorious and thrilling to have someone be jealous over what she did. But she now found that she wanted Sloan as a true friend more than as a jealous ex-lover. She resented him for all his warnings about "not getting hurt." She wanted to handle this herself.

Andrea walked past Jason's Café, already filling up with its evening crowd. The singles bars and cafés were the one aspect of her neighborhood that Andrea really disliked. It wasn't so much the fact that they existed as the fact that they drove other restaurants and bars out of business. Now it was impossible to get a chicken salad sandwich at a neighborhood restaurant without paying as much as you'd pay for a whole chicken in a grocery store; and a cup of coffee or a mug of beer were equally outrageous.

Andrea was just noticing a striking-looking blonde who was laughing so loudly that everyone at Jason's was staring at her, when she noticed the back of the man the blonde was sitting with at an outdoor table.

And she knew it was Jim. His shoulders — their size and the way he held them — were what made her so sure. And when he shook his head, probably embarrassed because the woman was causing such a commotion, she recognized the way he moved, and suddenly she felt as if she were back in ninth grade watching Jim walk out onto the field and wishing she had the nerve to just try to be a cheerleader. All of her confidence, all of her experience, everything was gone and in their place was horrible insecurity.

She was standing ten feet away from him, and she could either walk past and hope he didn't notice, or cross First Avenue in the middle of the street.

She felt utterly ridiculous: it had been a long time since she had tried to sneak past anyone, and it had been a longer time since she had felt so undone, so confused about what to do without even knowing why. All she knew was that she didn't want to see Jim right now — not while he was with another woman and their relationship was so up in the air. And she didn't want him to see her.

She turned away and stepped down off the curb between two parked cars, and she started to walk out into the street.

And then she heard, "Andrea!"

She hesitated.

"Andrea! Over here!"

She turned around. Jim was waving.

CHAPTER FOUR

Now the blonde he was with had turned too.

Andrea stood, motionless, but Jim was already up on his feet and coming toward her.

"Andrea," he said again. He pushed his way past a couple who were trying to read the menu that was posted on a sandwich board on the sidewalk, and then he was standing in front of her. "Come on over and sit down," he said casually, as if he hadn't stormed out of her office only a few hours ago.

"I'm on my way home," she said — lamely, she realized as soon as she had said it. But she still hadn't gotten herself back under control. The situation was reminiscent of so long ago. . . .

"One drink with your favorite and most cooperative client?" he prodded, mischief glinting brightly in his eyes. "Come on," he urged, and took her hand.

Andrea didn't want to make a scene. She didn't want to yank out of his grasp, and her curiosity about the woman sitting at

Jim's table was beginning to get the better of her. She followed him to the table.

But the moment she got there she realized she had made a mistake. In Jim's eyes she could see he already felt the afternoon's episode could be put aside — and he seemed merely to be taking pleasure in the fact that he had two women at the table now.

"Claudia, this is Andrea Sutton, the woman I was telling you about the other night."

Cute. Andrea thought. *So now he's let me know Claudia was with him the other night.*

"And Andrea, this is Claudia Cashman."

Claudia shot Jim a black look, and Jim and Andrea sat down.

Jim turned to Andrea. "Mad at me for this afternoon?"

"I'd rather not discuss it here," Andrea said quietly.

"Why? No one's listening." He turned to Claudia. "I made a colossal tactical error with Andrea and her partner today," he explained. "They offered me a part, or a chance at one, that I should have jumped at, and —"

"Jim," Andrea interrupted.

He looked at her with dancing pleasure in his eyes, as if to say, Aren't you glad I've changed my mind? "What's wrong?" he asked innocently.

"I asked you not to discuss business here."

He blinked. "I didn't think you were serious."

She looked at him skeptically. Wasn't he carrying his amused innocence routine just a little too far? "I was and am serious. You ought to see why."

He shrugged. "All right, whatever you say. I'll get us some drinks. What'll you have?" he asked, looking only at Andrea.

"Uh, a Campari and soda."

"Okay, one C and S coming up. Claudia?"

Claudia suddenly stood up. "Nothing for me, thanks," she bit out. "I didn't realize you had another . . . meeting, Jim. Good-bye."

"Claudia?"

But she was already threading her way between the tables and clearly wasn't about to turn around.

"You really know how to make everyone happy, don't you?" Andrea said.

"You mean Claudia?"

"Oh, come on! Claudia, me, Sloan, you, what have you done today that's been right?"

He held up his palms. "Hey, listen, Andrea, I just asked you to come sit down for a drink. I didn't know everyone would get so upset." He really hadn't been able to watch her walk by Jason's without jumping out of his seat to catch her.

"Oh, you didn't? I think you did. Or if you didn't, Jim, you should have. What did you expect? That Claudia would be *glad* you brought me over? Or that I would automatically forget all of those things you said this afternoon? You were obviously on a date; didn't you give that some kind of thought?"

"I was trying to be liberated," he said weakly. "I wanted to see you, all right? I wasn't going to let you walk away."

"Well, I don't blame Claudia for leaving," she said, although secretly she had to admit that at one level Claudia's leaving hadn't bothered her at all. "Anyway, it's just as well that I ran into you because I can tell you what I did."

He battled a handsome smile as his mesmerizing blue eyes shone. "What did you do?"

"I left the script off with your doorman, and I want you to read it tonight whether you want to or not."

He nodded slowly. "All right. I will," he said quietly.

"You will?"

"Don't look so surprised. A man can change his mind, you know. And I think that I *should* read the script."

She gazed into his eyes. "What made you change your mind?"

"Oh, it was a not very nice combination of things that happened this afternoon, I guess." He paused as the waiter set down their drinks, and he took a sip of beer before talking again. "It started with Claudia calling and wanting to go out and my saying yes just because I didn't want to be alone or even in my apartment. I haven't been a whole lot of fun to be with lately, especially with her, and I realized a little too late this afternoon that I've been doing that with everyone and everything. I'm so damned nervous about this career thing that it's got me all turned around. I was really thinking of you as a female Owen today."

"Thanks a lot," she said, smiling.

"Well, let's say a very attractive female Owen," he added, answering her smile with a grin. "I really didn't trust you. When you told me about this great part, the first thing I thought of was a starring role." He shook his head. "I know it sounds ridiculous, but that's what I thought. You and Sloan are supposed to work miracles and I thought, Great. It's my turn. Then when you explained what it was, I thought, Hell, the bull is starting again." He sighed. "Anyway, I'd love to read the script and I probably would have been too damned proud to ask for it, so I'm glad you brought it. I have only one complaint though."

"What's that?"

He smiled. "Why is my luck so rotten? The one time you come to my apartment I'm not even home!"

She raised a brow. "Well, you were with Claudia, Jim. I'm glad you weren't home."

"We met here, not at my house," he said quickly.

"You don't have to defend yourself," she said. "You're allowed to have a private life, you know."

"Yeah, well, that has to end. The thing with Claudia, I mean." He looked into Andrea's eyes. "Do you ever find that being nice to people is the worst thing you can do?"

"What do you mean?"

"Well, take Claudia for instance." He thought this was as good a time as any to let Andrea know it was over between Claudia and himself. "Our relationship has been pretty much over for a couple of weeks now. I haven't been much fun to be around, and she knows it and I know it, and we both know that part of the reason is that there isn't all that much between us anymore. And I know she wants to try to keep it going. So I've been pretending to look the other way." He shrugged. "I guess it seemed easier and nicer. Kinder. But it's not kinder or nicer or easier in the end. I've got to tell her it's over." He looked at Andrea, and his eyes were questioning. He took another sip of beer. "Do you agree?" he asked, taking a chance.

She hesitated. The moment seemed so charged. He seemed so near, with his warm knee nearly touching hers, his hand next to hers on the table, his eyes looking into hers exactly as she imagined they would if he were making love to her.

Yet she couldn't help also wondering if he was playing, leading her on as he had at the office, only to switch gears at the worst moment.

"*Do* you?" he repeated softly.

She shrugged, trying to lighten the mood. "It depends what you want."

"What if I want to be free?" he murmured.

She could remember the roughness of his cheeks, the warmth of his lips, the urgency of his tongue as he sought his pleasure. As she looked into his eyes she was trapped by their intensity, by the fantasy that she was already in bed with him, that he was telling her he loved her and would always love her, that he would be hers forever. As if she were really experiencing it, she could feel his rough hands warming her thighs, the honeyed warmth he'd bring to her burning core, the strength of his thrusts.

But then she remembered what they were talking about. She thought — and hoped — that he was saying he wanted to be free to go out with her. But he had played so many games. He had approached her and she had said no, he had approached her and then backed off, and she still didn't know whether he was using her for the sake of his career or not.

There was only one thing she was sure of. He wanted her as much as she wanted him, if only in a purely physical sense.

"Do you think that's a good idea, Andrea? My breaking up with Claudia, I mean?"

She didn't like the way he seemed to be manipulating her, forcing her to say things she wasn't sure of. "I really think you have to make that kind of decision for yourself."

He said nothing, leaning back in his chair and letting his gaze rest on her face. Damn, she was beautiful. Her eyes were a green like nothing he had ever seen before. And those lips. How many times had he held back from leaning over and covering them with his? There were times — like a little while ago — when he could swear she wanted him, when he could feel the heat that was burning between them as if it were fire. But then she'd say something — like now — that showed him she wasn't ready, or that she wanted him but wouldn't go through with it.

And it made him wonder if being together would totally mess up their professional relationship, just as she had said it would. He didn't believe it, and he would never let that kind of thinking stop him. But even if she was wrong, as long as she *thought* she was right, then just thinking it could make it come true. You could go up to home plate and use a bat the guys said was jinxed, and damned if you didn't get struck out in a minute and a half or less. If it turned out the bat was just a plain old bat, so what? It might as well have been jinxed. And it was the same with Andrea: he wanted her to know it was right between them, and to know she was ready and didn't care about anything else. Until then it didn't matter how much he wanted her — if she came to him before she was ready, she'd be sure to spoil the relationship good and fast. And he didn't want that.

But couldn't he try to change her mind?

"Look," he said quietly. "You talked about that acting lady — that coach — being willing to see me next week. But what about before then? Who's going to help me get ready for the audition?"

"Look, you haven't even read the script yet, Jim, so —"

He grinned. "I'm turning over a new leaf and putting all my trust in you, Andrea, with the guarantee — and remember, I said guarantee — that I'll be your favorite client by the end of the month."

"Oh, really?" she asked doubtfully, smiling. "That's a pretty tall order. Sloan and I have a lot of clients. We must —"

"I'm not talking about Sloan," he cut in. "I'm talking about you."

"Ah. I see. Well, what will you get if you win?"

He smiled. "Don't worry. That will be reward enough right there."

"And what if *I* win? What if you're not my favorite client?"

He shrugged. "That's easy. I'll quit."

"What? Jim, don't be ridiculous."

"I don't think it's that ridiculous. If I did, I wouldn't be making the bet."

She smiled and shook her head. "You're crazy. But in a week or two when you've forgotten all about the bet, I just won't remind you, and that'll be that. If I thought you were serious, you know, I'd be a little concerned."

"Why? I *am* serious."

"But Jim, that's just silly — it's exactly like expecting to start off in a starring role. I mean, it isn't *exactly* analogous, because being someone's favorite client isn't that wonderful. But the point is, why do you always have to be number one? This is a new career for you. The beginning. Can't you relax?"

He smiled. Andrea was often right, but in this case she was entirely wrong. Wanting to be her favorite client had absolutely nothing to do with his career. "All right," he agreed finally. "I'll relax if you promise to help me with those lines."

"It's a deal," she said, smiling. "And I was planning to anyway. I often work with clients on things like that even if they do have coaches."

"Then let's get started. Are you free?"
"You mean now?"
"I'm not talking about New Year's Eve, Andrea. Yes, now. We can have dinner at my house. If that's all right with you."
When his eyes met hers her breath caught, her heart skipped, and she felt like melting into his arms. "That sounds fine," she murmured.
"A couple of steaks, more cold beer than I think you'll be able to put away, and salad — okay?"
"Great," she said. Probably slated for Claudia though. She wished she could forget about her. But she knew Jim too well. She remembered when the one friend of hers who had gone out with him in high school came to her in tears one afternoon during study hall. Jim had missed their date the night before, and then she had overheard someone else, a new girl in school, talking about her date with Jim. The girl, Helen, had gone up to him and yelled, and he had been so horrified and convincingly sorry, swearing he had forgotten and swearing he'd make it up to her — that she had ended up saying yes to another date with him when what she really wanted was to tell him to go to hell. Andrea remembered her friend saying,

"But when I looked into his eyes, Andy, it was all over. I couldn't say anything but yes."

Now Jim was playing a little game with her. In his smoothest voice he asked her if he should break up with Claudia. With his most irresistible grin he told her he wanted to be her favorite client, giving her a very deep and arousing sense of the implications. And now he was telling her that the evening at his apartment could be much more than a simple script-reading.

Jim paid, joking and flirting with the waitress and giving a thumbs-up to a fan who had spotted him. Then he and Andrea began walking up First Avenue. It was the first time Andrea had been on the street with Jim, and she was pleased at the number of people who recognized him. That boded well for his new career.

When she mentioned this to him, he shrugged. "It all depends on the mood I'm in. I wouldn't have believed this if anyone else had told me, but when I'm feeling really rotten or sick or whatever, I could walk down the street in an Ace uniform and I swear no one would pay any attention to me. Now, though, with one of the world's top personal managers at my side, I feel like a king and *everyone* sees me."

She smiled, but his words also made her wonder whether he thought of her more as a manager or as a woman. In a rather disturbing way it went along with his wanting to be her favorite client.

They got to his building and picked up the script, and Andrea was soon surprised to see — as Jim opened the door to his apartment — that many of her negative observations and assumptions about his building had been wrong. She had been expecting to find the usual Upper East Side hideously expensive box disguised as a four- or five-room apartment. What Jim brought her to, though, was entirely different. Even from the foyer Andrea could see a beautiful terrace beyond the living room, with a magnificent view that swept across the East River. And as Jim showed her around the apartment she was more and more impressed with what he had done. He had transformed what could have been a very plain space into one that beautifully and strongly reflected his own tastes. The living room looked like a western lodge, with Navajo rugs, large, cushioned sofas covered with sunset-hued fabrics, paintings that spoke of the Old West and wide-open spaces. The kitchen was what she would have expected: slightly messy and very lived-in-looking, and Jim looked a bit embarrassed as he showed it to her.

"My favorite room," he said laughingly as they looked into the bedroom. It was lovely, with the same western flavor as the living room: the curtains, rugs, and bedspread were all of rust-toned fabrics and watercolors of the Canadian wilderness were on the walls.

She glanced in at the bathroom as they left, curious more because she wanted to know where it was than because she expected to find anything interesting. But she saw a glint of pink-gold marble and a flash of chrome, and she knew what she had seen. "A Jacuzzi?" she asked, smiling.

He shrugged and grinned. "Hey, listen, I had to live up to the image."

"Mmm. I'll bet."

"And here's my second favorite room," he said, putting a warm hand at her waist as he opened a door.

It was an exercise room — small but as well-equipped as some gyms Andrea had seen — with a Nautilus at the center of the room and a lot of strange-looking contraptions on the walls.

"Jim, I can't believe you have all this in your apartment!"

"Do you like it?" he asked.

"I don't know. It makes me feel guilty just looking at it. All that equipment seems to be saying, You vowed to join a gym this year, Andrea Sutton, and you *still* haven't done it!"

He laughed. "Well, you're welcome to use this stuff anytime you want. Though you certainly don't need it." His gaze swept over her figure, taking in her breasts and the delicious curve of her waist and hips that he hadn't been able to forget, her long slender legs he knew well in his dreams, in his fantasies. If only . . .

"How about another drink?" he asked.

"Sure."

"Okay, follow me," he said, holding out a hand.

When she took his hand it was warm and persuasive in an oddly low-key way that was very sexy. Jim seemed to be definitely up to something — acting ambiguously and backing off whenever she expected him to take her in his arms. Teasing, almost. As he walked through the living room to the bar, his pace was slow and languid, a hip daring her to brush against it, the subtle pressure of his thumb in her palm daring her to resist. And underneath there was a deeper dare: It's your turn, he seemed to be saying, as he seemed to have been saying since he had told her they should wait. And that was unsettling, not because she was opposed to the woman making the first move, but because with Jim it seemed to be part of a game. It was as if he wanted her to make the first move not because he found that idea sexy or appealing, but because she had told him no, and her advance would be like a signed slip of paper saying, I was wrong. Take me. I want you even though I know it's a bad idea, even though I know you're unreliable, even though I know you'll break my heart. And she wasn't ready to make that kind of blind leap.

They stepped up to the bar — a modern structure near the terrace doors in the living room — and Jim looked at Andrea with those infuriating bedroom eyes again. "Another Campari and soda?"

"Please." She tore herself away from Jim's gaze — much too dangerous at the moment — but was immediately captivated by him again, this time in a photograph of him with a young woman.

"Who's that with you in the picture?" she asked.

He glanced at it and smiled. "That's my sister — the one I was telling you about."

Andrea went over to the photograph and picked it up — two extraordinarily good-looking people with a family resemblance that was difficult to detect. Katie's eyes were as brown as Jim's were blue, her features delicate where his were bold, and her hair stick-straight where his was wavy. "You really don't look anything at all alike."

He smiled. "Lucky Katie. What girl wants to look like a first baseman with the Aces? Or worse yet, an *ex*-first baseman? The nice thing, though, is that we're so far apart in years that I can really be a friend to her." He shook his head. "And it just makes me so damn mad to see what's happening to her now."

"It's really too bad," Andrea said. "She looks like a nice kid."

"She is," he said. "And the reason that what she's going through is driving me so crazy is because I remember that feeling of rejection so well. It's the same reason I was so rotten to you this afternoon. I don't want to sound like I feel sorry for myself because I know there are millions of people who've had it so much harder than I have — but still, I'll never forget those three times I was sent down to the minors, and all those other times before that, when

I'd get passed over for my first chance at the majors. It's kind of hard to explain, but I really felt as if my whole life was tied into whether I was accepted or not. And even when I saw that life did go on, the next time I was rejected I would feel the same way all over again. And I can see that Katie feels that way."

"But she's just starting out," Andrea objected. "I mean, I know how she must feel — I remember the feeling myself — but she's only eighteen."

"Well, all I know is that she feels it's the end of the world. And I feel like mowing down everyone who's responsible for her unhappiness." He handed Andrea her drink and then raised his own. "But I really didn't bring you here to talk about Katie and her job struggles — or me and my past, Andrea." His eyes found hers. "Or even to read the script," he added softly. "I want to apologize for the way I've been acting." He reached out and gently cupped her cheek in his warm hand. "I've never forgotten that dark-haired beauty I met all those years ago, and I've been taking advantage of who you are . . . the kind of person you are . . . and acting like whatever the male version of a prima donna is. What is it, anyway?"

She smiled. "I don't know. But I know what you're saying. And I promise you it happens to just about everyone."

He shook his head. "Not what *I'm* feeling, Andrea. At least I hope not. I know what you've said other times, about the way clients end up thinking they're great stars and all that. But that's not what I'm talking about. I don't want to be grouped with all your other clients." He reached out and touched the bare skin of her arm, his hand warming her and making her remember. . . .

"Andrea, I've been fighting myself for days, ever since we were in your office and I told you" — he grinned — "fool that I was, that I thought we should go more slowly. I don't want to force you into something you don't want. But I can't play games anymore." He shook his head. "I had decided I'd try to make you want me no matter what it took — game-playing included. But I don't want to play games with you anymore. I don't want to pretend. I want you, and I want to try to make you see that I'm not the person you think I am. If I could have you, if I could make love with you, how could I want another woman?"

He brought her into his arms and gazed

at her, and his eyes — deep and blue and giving — said more than words could. He looked so tender, so sincere. And his nearness, his scent, the strength of his hold as he splayed his hands over her hips, the hardness of his frame she remembered so well — all were deeply arousing.

"I know what you've said, Andrea, that it would be too complicated if we were lovers, that it couldn't work out." His lips were brushing against hers then, filling her with the memory of his other kisses, filling her with the memory of dreams in which he had been the most magnificent lover. "But I want to take that chance. And I wish I could make you see . . ." His voice trailed off, and his lips took over as they covered hers and the kiss deepened.

Oh, how she wanted him. He kissed her neck, the throbbing pulse at its base, the cool skin beneath the silk of her dress, and she knew what it would be like to feel those kisses everywhere, to feel the tenderness of his persuasion and the hard strength of his need, to hear him urge her on to pleasure that would be deeper than any she had ever felt.

As he unbuttoned the front of her dress and parted the fabric, she watched as his eyes darkened with pleasure, as he lowered his lips with a moan and covered a nipple with his wet mouth. She wrapped her arms around him, loving the feel of her fingers in his soft hair and the strength of his shoulders, moaning as he brought each nipple to a peak.

"I want you so much," he whispered as he laid her back on the couch and gazed down at her. "I want to show you — to make you see how good it could be . . ." His fingers roved down her stomach and over her hips, teasing at the band of her bikini and then moving on, down her thighs, where his lips soon followed, where his hot wet kisses filled her with a desperate hunger. His tongue teased and played, suggesting in the deepest ways all the pleasures he could give her, and when he slid off her shoes and began to work his way back up her legs, leaving a trail of warm kisses along her calves, her knees, her inner thighs, she was awash with a burning desire that only he could satisfy. A picture flashed in her mind — Jim in the centerfold, his eyes saying he wanted her and his body showing how he could satisfy her, how he could fill her with his hard strength and slake her throbbing inner need. She remembered the way his chest had looked — broad, masterful, with hardened nipples made for teasing, muscles she wished she could cover with kisses. She remembered his thighs — lean, hard, covered with fine dark hair, and she remembered his slim hips, his firm buttocks, his beautiful sex.

And she wanted him. As he reached the edge of her bikinis with his tongue and began pulling them down with each hand, she desperately wanted him, knowing deep in her heart that nothing else mattered at that moment except making love with this magnificent man.

He knelt above her, warming her as he gazed down at her naked form, and then he tore off his shirt and stood up to take off the rest of his clothes. She rose and helped him, sliding off his shoes and undoing his pants, running her hands over his beautiful form and then kneeling as she slowly slid off his last remaining garment. She kissed his hard thighs, the lean slopes of his hips, the center line of hair going down his stomach, and then he pulled her up so they were both standing, looking into each other's eyes.

She thought he looked more exquisite in that moment than she had ever seen him, just gazing at her and saying all he needed to say with his eyes.

And then he swept her into his arms and carried her across the soft carpeting of the living room.

He brought her into the softly lit bedroom and laid her down on the satin quilt, and he looked down at her as she gazed at him. He was more amazed by her beauty than ever. When had she turned into such a knockout? She had always been pretty, but in high school she was slim almost to the point of skinniness. Now she was voluptuous, her breasts full, her hips the most perfectly curving he had ever seen, her waist delicate, and her legs long and slender. And her coloring was magnificent — pale skin, a mane of dark hair, skin that was always satin-smooth and scented.

He climbed onto the bed and knelt above her and then stretched himself out beside her, and slowly, holding back a male need he could barely control, he began to make her his. He sank his lips to her breasts, delighting in their soft fullness, the peaked nipples that rose so readily to his tongue and the gentle tug of his teeth. He ran his hands in wonder over her curves, knowing that someday he'd explore every inch of her body with his lips, his tongue, his soul. Under the heat of his touch

Andrea was amazed that she had ever been able to say no to this man; she had sensed his tenderness from the beginning, and now he was showing her, with slowly spiraling speed, how wildly exciting such tenderness could be. His warm hands trailed over the length of her thighs and in between, teasing and suggesting, daring her to resist. As she arched herself in need, his touch grew more urgent, his own quickened breathing a match for her sighs and moans. As she fell more and more deeply under the spell of his heated strength, his obvious male need, she ground her fingers into his shoulders, his back, his buttocks, and together their bodies grew wet with perspiration and heat.

Jim was amazed at the fierceness of Andrea's responses, the depth with which she gave herself.

And when he moved on top of her, whispering her name and gazing down at her, he knew the time was right, that neither one could wait any longer, that his need was too great for anything but complete satisfaction. And he kissed her deeply, covering her lips and tasting of her sweetness, and as she nibbled at his lips, his neck, his ear, he claimed her hips with his and brought the two of them together with a powerful thrust. Andrea couldn't believe the hot pleasure, the way he filled her so completely with such deep, stroking love. He brought her higher and higher until she was sure there could be no greater pleasure, and then he'd bring her higher still, biting at her wet shoulder, hoarsely grating her name, taking her with him to a place she had never been. And then as she cried out he unleashed his passion completely and rocked them both to the core with shattering pleasure.

It was minutes before they moved as they lay sated in each other's arms. Andrea felt as if she had awakened from a dream, as if no pleasure could ever have been as deep as this was.

She nuzzled her lips into the warmth of his neck and sighed happily. "You're magnificent," she whispered.

He turned and looked into her eyes. "Only with you, darling. I can't believe . . ."

His voice drifted off, and she smiled. "What?"

"That we're so good together."

Her smile faded, though she tried to hide it. Was it possible that his feelings for her could be so strong? Would they last?

Suddenly she was panicked about the future. She had thrown away all her rules, turned away from the fears and suspicions that had warned against her getting emotionally involved with Jim. Now it was too late, but she'd never forget the joy, the sheer ecstasy of being with him. She didn't want to ever forget them. She was old enough now to recognize someone very special, an experience and a man wonderful enough to change her entire life. But was he?

CHAPTER FIVE

Over the next few days life was pure joy for Andrea. She worked hard every day and spent every night — blissfully — with Jim. Her fears about the relationship dissolved more each night as she got to know Jim better and realized he wasn't treating the relationship casually. He had broken up with Claudia as kindly as had been possible, and had told Andrea that for the first time ever, all aspects of his life seemed to be heading m the right direction. Andrea went to his house and he to hers, and each night, at the end of the evening, he'd make her promise she'd be with him the next night. For Andrea, it was a very silly question. How could she not want to spend her time with this wonderful man?

As he took her face in his strong hands and gazed into her eyes, as he brushed his loving lips against hers and murmured softly that he wouldn't be able to get through the next day without knowing he'd see her that night, she knew she had never felt this way about anyone. Being with Jim was pure pleasure, and with every night came a deeper pleasure as they grew to know each other more intimately.

They worked hard too. He had auditioned for and been accepted by Olga Rafelson, and was a member of her group classes as well as her private ones. But each night Andrea worked on his lines too. Without either of them acknowledging it, both knew that the audition for the part of Kyle Whiting would be among the most important of Jim's career. Not because it was an excellent part, or even because it would be for an Alexander and Eva Kropotkin production, but because it would be the first part he would try out for under Andrea's management, and it would in a sense be a portent of all that would come in the future. Andrea knew that putting so much importance on a part — on *any* part — was dangerous and unwise. But was there any way to prevent it?

After she and Jim had gone over his reading for the fourth night in a row, she put her arms around him as they sat on the couch and she looked into his beautiful eyes. "I know how much this part means to you," she said quietly.

"Well, hell, Andrea, it's a great part."

"But listen to me. Don't get your heart set on it."

He didn't blink. "Why not? Has something happened? Did the producers call?"

"No. But I just don't want to see you disappointed. That's all."

"You don't think I can do it?"

"I think you can do it, Jim. I wouldn't be working with you if I didn't. But sometimes things fall through, and you should know that. Remember, it isn't definite."

"I know that," he said slowly, untwining her arms from his shoulders. He leaned forward and lit a cigarette. When he put the lighter back on the coffee table, he turned and looked at Andrea. "You make me damned jittery when you talk like this, Andrea. I was all set to go."

"Oh, come on. Don't blame me. If one tiny thing can set you off, then you aren't ready. Don't you see? I had to say something. The way we've both been acting these past four or five days it's as if we're in a world in which nothing matters except this part."

He smiled. "And each other. What's the matter with that?"

"It's unrealistic. And it's dangerous. I don't want to see you disappointed."

He looked surprised. "But I will be disappointed if I don't get the part. I don't believe in that business of pretending you won't get something so you'll get used to the idea of failure. That doesn't work, and it's a waste of time. Anyway, Andrea, I promise I can take care of myself."

But she wondered. Would he blame her if he didn't get the part? How much of the success of their relationship depended on Jim's professional success? Andrea was afraid to look too deeply.

On the eighth night, two nights before the date of the audition, Andrea noticed something new — and wrong — in Jim's reading. "Wait a minute," she said after he had finished a line.

He looked annoyed. "What's the matter?"

"Why did you change it?" she asked. "You're supposed to be Lynda Palmer's secret lover — not the commander of a SWAT team."

"What's that supposed to mean?" His voice was rough with annoyance.

"You're supposed to be seducing her, Jim, smoothly, and with just a hint of evil, not a whole ton of it."

He didn't say anything. But she could see anger in his eyes, see the tightness of his jaw. And when he finally spoke, it was as if it were all he could do not to yell. "I've been studying night and day for this damned role, Andrea. I'm taking private classes with Olga Rafelson, group classes with Olga Rafelson and a dozen other actors, going over my lines with you, *and* going over them by myself. I think I know the scene better than anyone I'm working with at this point, and I think I know what it needs."

"But you're wrong!" she cried. "Look, I think it's great that you're taking rehearsing so seriously. But I've got to tell you it was a lot better — a hell of a lot better — last night."

"Did you discuss this aspect of the scene with the Kropotkins?" he asked.

"No, I didn't. But if you're trying to say you know more about the part than I do, don't bother. I've worked with the Kropotkins a lot. I know the script, and I know what they want. Please, Jim, believe me. I don't want to see you mess this up."

He reached for a cigarette and then threw it back on the table, muttering something about smoking too much lately. Then he turned to Andrea. "This is damned hard for me, you know," he said hoarsely. "I just can't get used to it."

"You mean my being your manager?"

He shrugged. "Managing is okay. If you were doing what Owen did — without all the lying and crap like that — I would think it was fine. But this business of working so closely together" — his eyes found hers — "it just can't work if you're always right, if you always know more than I do."

"But I don't," she said softly. "Don't you see that you're the prize? You're the treasure? You're what this is all about. My job — and Olga Rafelson's job — wouldn't even exist without people like you." She smiled. "And there is one area in which you happen to be the world's leading expert — it's called pleasing me, Jim, knowing how to make me feel . . ." Her voice trailed off as he brought her close and gazed into her eyes. "Feel wonderful," she finally finished, mesmerized by his nearness. "You have to know that that's true no matter what else happens between us," she murmured.

"Darling," he whispered, gently massaging the back of her neck, running searching fingers through the softness of her hair. "If I could know I pleased you more than any other man . . . if I could know that . . . it would make everything else so much less important."

His lips were close now, his rough cheek scratchy against hers, the musky smell of his cologne making her warm and tingly. The feel and smell of him so close triggered a physical memory that was deeply arousing. The heat spread through her limbs as she remembered his shouts of pleasure and triumph, the way he had held back what was obviously throbbing need until he knew she was ready, the way his flaming strokes of love had merged them into one blaze of passion.

As she looked into his magnificent blue eyes she felt drunk with the pleasure of anticipation, the pleasure of knowing he wanted her, that he wanted to please her and knew so well how to do that.

When he reached out and grasped her thigh, the heat of his warm hand burned through the silk of her dress, and she covered his hand with hers.

"Oh, God, Andrea, I want this to work between us," he whispered. "I want you so much."

He brushed his lips against her, and the touch was like a dream, tender and sweet and persuasive at the same time.

And with the grace of lovers meant to be together, they melted into each other's arms, undressing each other with touches that caressed here and teased there, sighs of wanting and delight mixing with delicate kisses against damp skin.

When Jim was naked and stretched out before her, Andrea gazed in wonder at him, amazed, as she always was, at the perfection of his body. He was all sinew and muscle, all strength and lean power. As she knelt beside him and ran her fingers over the contours of his chest, he reached out and touched her breasts, cupping each one with a warm hand and teasing her nipples with his thumbs. Her response was immediate as desire shot through her and made her tingle under his touch.

"You're so beautiful," he whispered. "And when I'm away from you I'm certain I can remember how lovely you are. And then when I see you . . ." His voice trailed off as he rose up and laid her back on the couch. "And it gives me so much pleasure to please you," he murmured as he lowered his head and covered her lips with his own.

She opened to him immediately, warming to the pleasures of his coaxing tongue and his hand as it roved down from her breasts to her hips to her thighs. He knew what pleased her, he knew what made her writhe with desire, and he was obviously taking his time, making her pleasure all the sweeter by drawing it out.

He tore his mouth from hers and gazed down at her with eyes that were burning with passion. "All those years we've wasted. How many years was it?"

She smiled. "Twelve."

"Twelve years," he said huskily, covering her hips with a hard thigh. "Twelve long years," he grated. "Well, tonight, darling, I'm going to try to make up for twelve long years."

He lowered his lips to a breast, gently kissing one nipple and then the other, teasing one and then the other with the quivering tip of his wet tongue. And he moved above her, shifting so his warm fingers teased and circled and seared her thighs and the dark triangle of silken hair between. Each time she thought she'd get that special touch he knew so well he'd deftly move away until she thought she wouldn't be able to stand it anymore. And then, as she was longing for his touch, he seared her with fingers that brought her to a point of flaming sensuality.

She clutched at him, loving the feel of his warm, wet back beneath her hands, feeling the heat coming from every part of his body. He was ready for her, fully aroused and ready to satisfy her, and she wanted him.

"Jim," she whispered. "Jim, darling."

He raised his head and looked into her eyes with blazing pleasure, then lightly teased his lips down the center of her stomach, down to the searing core of pleasure he was seeking with his hand. And he took possession of her then, deftly coaxing her with lashes of his tongue that rocked her with pleasure that knew no bounds. She was engulfed by a glow, by the fiery strokes that brought her higher and higher, and in a dizzying burst of fire she was his, trembling beneath him and then conscious of nothing but white-hot pleasure and bliss.

When she opened her eyes he began kissing her on one thigh and then on the other, showering her with kisses on each hipbone, on the soft skin of her stomach, on each breast, and then he gazed into her eyes with pleasure as his hand reached for the place he had just flooded with passion.

"Jim —"

"Andrea, it's so perfect between us, it's almost hard to believe," he said hoarsely. "I've never felt this way with any other woman. It's special between us, isn't it?"

But before she could answer he was

bringing her to the summit of pleasure again, where moans were easier than words and she could barely gasp his name.

And then he moved on top of her, his lean hips covering hers, and he brought them together with a thrust of fire, his hard strength filling her with the pleasure she craved. They moved quickly, convulsively, as he merged her with his passion, as his sweat mixed with hers and their needs grew deeper. His urging strokes brought them closer and closer to ecstasy until Andrea was engulfed once again, crying out with joy that was echoed in Jim's cries of pleasure.

They both lay there, spent and exhausted, in each other's arms, and when Andrea finally changed position, she had no idea how much time had passed. All she knew was that she couldn't imagine a time when she wouldn't love making love with Jim. Beyond that she didn't want to look into the future. For she suspected that nothing could stay this easy, this wonderful, for long.

The day before Jim's audition was scheduled Andrea called Jim from her office. They had already arranged to meet at his house that night, but she needed to ask him a question about Owen for their lawyer.

"Hey, Andrea," he said after they had exchanged hellos. "I just had a fantastic group class. You're talking to the A-number-one Stanley Kowalski of the day."

She laughed. "That's great. Listen, I have to ask you a question about Owen for our lawyer. Do you know if he kept any other offices? Like if he did business from an office or suite in California?"

"Well, he was always talking about his 'people.' He'd say, 'I'll get my people in L.A. on it right away,' or 'I'll get my people in Vegas to look into it.' But as far as I know, that was all bull. He definitely didn't have an address out there. I know because every time he went he stayed at different hotels, and I never had an office number I could contact him at."

"Hmm. That's interesting. Well, I'll tell our lawyer, and if there's anything else I need to know today, I'll let you know."

"Why do they want to know about other offices?" he asked.

"Oh, a lot of reasons. For one thing, it's important to know as much as you can in general about the other side. But it's also important to know if they go by other corporate names or if they're hiding their assets anywhere else. Or, for that matter, if they've sued before or been sued before under other names."

"But we're not suing Owen, he's suing us."

"Well, we may sue him in a countersuit. I just don't know yet."

He sighed. "I really didn't want all this to happen, you know. I just wanted to become an actor, not start being the sole support of the legal profession."

"Look, I'm sure it won't come to our countersuing. It's just an idea. Anyway, I've got a client waiting. But I'll see you tonight."

"Uh, actually, Andrea, something has come up."

"What?"

"Well, not something — just me. I need to be alone tonight to get myself geared up."

"You mean for the audition?"

"Yeah. I didn't realize it until this morning and I was going to call you. Anyway, I'm glad you called."

"Well, I understand," she said quietly. She was disappointed because she had wanted to spend the evening with him. But she was relieved, too, that tension was the only reason he wanted to call the evening off. When he had first said, "Something has come up," her stomach had felt like a hollow pit of fear, and she thought, *This is it, the relationship is over.* For a week now the relationship had been very intense — existing in a vacuum, with only the best feelings and the most passionate love-making. When they argued they made up by making love. When they missed each other they made up for it by making love. When they gazed into each other's eyes and Andrea thought she would never be happier than she was at that moment, Jim would prove her wrong as he'd bring her closer and show her how deep her happiness could be. And when, as she heard those words, "Something has come up," she thought she had lost him, she realized she had let her emotions run wild, pull her into a storm she hadn't intended even to get close to.

When Jim had first kissed her, she had sensed that whatever was between them would have to be all or nothing. His kiss was too tender and reached her too deeply; she knew he would be very special to her. And after that she had found herself trapped by thoughts of him, thinking about him at the oddest and most infuriating moments. But now all that seemed trivial.

There had been other men she had thought of nearly constantly, other men whose very names could plunge her into hours of fantasy. But with Jim her fantasies no longer seemed like idle dreams; she desperately wanted them to come true. And in the moments when she thought she had lost him, she saw for the first time how deeply she wanted and needed him, and that she loved him.

And she definitely hadn't planned for that to happen.

She ended the call by telling him to phone her if he wanted company, and he promised he would.

And she marveled at how dreams of so many years before were coming true. Yet she didn't feel secure. Because behind every fear she held about the relationship, yet another fear lurked: would her professional relationship with him destroy what they had? Would he ever feel as she did? She had set aside so many concerns; she had had to, because there was no choice. When you loved someone, how could you tell yourself to stop just because he seemed to be the type who was unreliable, or just because you knew you'd be hurt in the end, or that the relationship couldn't fit in with your professional plans for that person? Andrea hadn't been able to stop herself, and she had fallen for Jim more deeply every night. And the problems had grown silently beneath the surface, without her knowing or even thinking about them.

Tomorrow was the audition. And she had a sickening feeling that if Jim didn't get the part, their relationship — maybe even both parts of it — would end.

Jim set down his drink and walked to the edge of the terrace. Damn. Drinking Scotch in the afternoon. And alone, no less. He couldn't remember ever being this nervous. Not even in the World Series.

He smiled and shook his head. One little part. One lousy little part. Kyle Whiting in *The Princess of Destiny*. And he couldn't help feeling as if everything depended on his getting it.

Andrea was sweet to try to make him not care, but they both knew that the part of Kyle Whiting was more than just one great little part. It meant that his career would really begin, or that it wouldn't. And, damn it, he just couldn't visualize getting the part. In baseball he had learned a trick that had gotten to be second nature after a while: if you imagined yourself hitting a homer, if you really felt that bat connect and that ball fly, if you could hear the crowd roar and feel your legs carry you like the wind, you had a hell of a lot better chance of hitting a homer than if you dragged yourself up to the plate knowing you were going to strike out, that you had struck out last time you were up and you'd do it again. And he knew that the best thing he could do with this Kyle Whiting part was to assume he'd get it, to imagine the audition going fantastically, and imagine the Kropotkins, even though he had never seen them, congratulating him. But every time he thought of it, he saw himself all alone on a stage with a dry mouth, soaking-wet hands, rubber legs, and not a line in his head. When he thought about it he couldn't remember a single line. Nothing. There was no way he was going to get the part; he just knew it.

He finished the Scotch and chewed the ice, and set the glass down on the table next to the edge of the terrace. His hands were as wet as they had been in the daydream, and his legs were as weak.

A few minutes later he walked through the swinging doors at Jason's and waved to his friends at the bar.

Two hours later he was drunker than he

had been in years. He had an old girlfriend, Lisa, who was a Farouche model, on his left, a girlfriend of hers who was also a model and whose name he couldn't for the life of him remember on his right, and half the New York Aces on all sides at the bar. These were the guys he knew, who knew what he could do, and whom he didn't have to prove anything to. Same with the women too. His reputation was solid in here, and he didn't have to audition for anyone, damn it. They didn't even know about the audition; they had probably never even heard of the Kropotkins.

Kropotkins. Audition. The words were in the back of his mind, but so far back he shoved them out completely. With ease. And he drank some more.

At 1:00 a.m., when he was in the middle of what he drunkenly thought was the saddest story in the world — the story of how he hurt his arm and couldn't play ball anymore — he suddenly remembered what the next day was. Max, the bartender, had shut off the set over the bar when the late show had come on, and something in the music had made him remember. . . .

Nine fifteen. The audition was at nine fifteen. And it was 1:00 and he could hardly see. . . .

He shoved himself off the barstool and staggered to the door, leaving Lisa and Angela, the model whose name he finally remembered now that it was scrawled across the back of his hand, mystified and hurt, and his old buddies merely surprised. He was *the* Jim Haynes; they had all been sure he'd go home with Angela. What was the matter with him, they wondered.

First Avenue was a blur when Jim got outside. Streaks of light, cars whizzing by, men and women inexplicably lurching toward him. But he made it home, and he just managed to set his alarm clock before he passed out, utterly dead to the world.

The next morning, an uneasy queasiness hit Andrea the moment she awakened. She had slept badly. She had thought about Jim all evening and resisted calling, and then finally, at eleven, had given in and dialed his number. But all she got was his answering machine. Was he out, she had wondered, or was he asleep and just not picking up the phone?

Now, this morning, she was tempted to call just to say good luck. But she told herself to resist the impulse. He had told her he needed time and space to himself; it was a perfectly reasonable request, and she owed it to him to honor it. Still, she wished she knew what he was doing. . . .

When she arrived at work she looked at the *Times*'s arts and entertainment pages, as she always did, and then turned to the *News*'s gossip pages. Though most of the items in any of the newspapers were plain old news rather than really juicy gossip, it was still interesting — and imperative for Andrea — to read the daily tidbits that the stars' publicists had so carefully planted.

But when Andrea saw the picture at the top of page nine, she wasn't thinking about publicists or stars or anyone but Jim. There, in the same kind of fuzzy black and white picture that had been her only contact with Jim for years, was Jim himself, surrounded by men who looked vaguely familiar and flanked on either side by a beautiful woman, both of whom also looked familiar. Andrea stared at the picture. Jim looked handsome but smashed, with one eye half closed and a crooked smile she knew was a drunken one. Underneath, the caption read, "Teammates Tie Ten on after Trouncing Toronto," and there was a small article which said most of them had celebrated their victory against the Bluejays at Jason's the night before, with enough Farouche models around to seem like a photographer's dream-come-true. "Ex-Ace Jim Haynes, rumored to be embarking on an acting career (will he be our next big poster man?) helped his ex-teammates celebrate with obvious gusto."

Andrea put down the paper and picked up the phone. She looked at her watch and saw it was already 9:30; Jim's audition would probably just be getting started. But maybe he hadn't even made it to the Kropotkins' office! From his looks in the picture it would have been a miracle for him even to wake up.

His answering machine clicked on, and she hung up. He was either asleep or out. And she was so angry she almost didn't care which was true. All that work they had put in, those nights of rehearsing. And he had thrown it all away.

She had too much work that morning to allow herself to brood. A new client was coming at ten, and she had an important meeting with Sloan at eleven. But even so, she knew she wouldn't be able to stop thinking about what Jim had done. And what annoyed her more than anything else was that she was sure he wouldn't think he had done anything wrong, yet he would never have gone out and gotten that drunk before an important game or a tryout for a new team. He knew you couldn't be at your best if you had a hangover, yet he hadn't cared enough to prevent it. And now he'd lose out on a part they had both acknowledged as important.

Andrea's meeting with her new client, a young woman named Marina Heywood, only emphasized Jim's bad points. Marina had already been billed as the great star of the eighties by *Faces* magazine, and she had been on the covers of *Elle* and the Italian *Vogue* for years. And she was as professional and serious as Jim seemed to be unprofessional and frivolous.

In the middle of Andrea's next meeting with Sloan her intercom buzzed and Rachelle announced that Alexander Kropotkin was on the line.

Andrea thanked her and looked at Sloan. "Well, I'm braced for the bad news," she said, and pressed down the button. "Hello, Alex."

"Andrea, darling. You have sent me a genius."

"Excuse me?"

"Eva and I are thrilled with your Jim. He is our Kyle Whiting."

"Really? That's wonderful!" Sloan winked and she smiled. She was in a daze, absolutely amazed that Jim had gotten the part. She finished up the details of Jim's arrangements, and then hung up and shook her head. "Well, *he's* living under a lucky star. I really think —"

The intercom buzzed again, and Rachelle announced that Jim was in the reception area.

Sloan, looking displeased, glanced at his watch. "He must be early," he complained.

"I'm not even expecting him."

Sloan frowned. "Oh, what the hell. We're finished anyway," he muttered, and he rose abruptly from the table.

Andrea buzzed Rachelle and asked her to send Jim in, and a few moments later Sloan said a terse hello and left as Jim entered the office.

The moment Sloan shut the door Jim took Andrea in his arms. "Ask me how it went," he said happily, his blue eyes dancing with pleasure.

She didn't even smile. "I could ask you how last night went," she said flatly.

He looked confused. "Last night?"

She extricated herself from his grasp and went over to her desk, where she picked up the newspaper and opened to page nine. "*This* last night," she said. "Thursday night."

His eyes widened and then he smiled.

"Well, I'll be." He laughed. "I don't even remember when they took this picture. Let me see."

She grabbed the paper back from his grasp. "You can see it later," she snapped. "And I believe you when you say you don't remember that picture. You looked smashed to the gills."

He straightened and met her gaze. "I was," he said simply. "What is this, the third degree? I don't remember promising I'd be with you every night."

"I wasn't talking about that. I'm talking about getting drunk the night before an audition. Hours before the audition actually."

"I can't believe it! Are you serious? I needed to blow off some steam. I wanted to be with people who talked about something other than auditions and callbacks and agents and all that other crap I've been hearing all week at my acting class. And you're saying — what? That I should have stayed home and bitten my nails all night?"

"You could have called me."

"I didn't want to call you!" he exploded. "Damn it, you're exactly who I didn't want to call! Don't you understand? I had to get out from under you. If we were just seeing each other, it would be different. But that's not the way it is."

"I understand that you're living under a damned lucky star to have gotten that part after what you did. You —" It was only when she saw the look of astonishment on his face that she realized what she had said.

"I got the part?"

She sighed. "Yes, you got the part."

"And you didn't tell me?" His voice was rough with anger.

She looked him in the eyes. "You are not the one who has the right to be angry right now, Jim, so don't pull that non—"

"I don't have the right?" he roared. "What the hell kind of manager is it who doesn't tell her client when he gets a part?"

"What the hell kind of client is it who goes out and nearly blows his chances on something he and his manager have been working so damned hard on?" she seethed.

"I'd just like to know when you were planning on telling me I had gotten the part. *If* you were planning on telling me, that is."

"What's that supposed to mean?" she demanded.

"Just what it sounds like, Andrea. There's someone in this room who has a lot of explaining to do, and it's not me."

"Ah. I see," she said sarcastically. "And what if you hadn't gotten the part? Would you have blamed yourself just a little bit because you'd know that being hung over didn't help?"

"I don't have to listen to this," he said roughly. "You sound more like my mother than my manager. Except that my mother hasn't talked to me like that for fifteen years."

"Well, someone needs to, Jim, and I'm really sorry it has to be me because I promise you I don't like it one bit. But this is what it's like being managed, and you asked for it. You're the one who wants your career to go perfectly from square one, and you're the one who said you were used to being coached. And I know you accepted having a coach when you were in baseball, because you had to. So what about now?"

His eyes were unreadable. "I really don't know," he said quietly. "I don't really understand how you work, Andrea. I go out, I have a few drinks, I have an audition I'm really excited about, and I come to tell you about it. Then you yell at me for going out, and you don't even tell me I've gotten the part. To me that sounds like there's something very wrong. And I don't see why it has to be that way."

"Then maybe you'd better think this whole thing through and see if you want to continue."

For a moment, as she spoke, she saw the darkness of pain in his eyes, a sadness that made her want to take back her words.

"Think about what whole thing?" he asked quietly.

"Your career and my managing it," she said, wanting to soften her tone but resisting at the same time. She didn't want to fall victim to those magical eyes, to start compromising when she knew she was right. "I know I'm going to think about whether I want to continue this."

"We have a contract," he said flatly.

"It can be broken. There are clauses."

His jaw tightened. "You're really something," he said quietly. For one moment his eyes burned into hers. Then he turned and walked out the door, slamming it loudly behind him.

CHAPTER SIX

Jim stood in a phone booth at the corner of Ninety-third and Second, waiting for his sister's phone to answer. The booth stank, and the October cool had vanished with the noon sun. Jim felt that just fit, considering the way everything else was going. Hell, he didn't even feel good about getting the Kyle Whiting part.

A few minutes later, though, as he raced up the stairs to the fifth-floor walkup apartment Katie shared with another girl, he began to feel better. Seeing his sister always made him feel good and made him remember there were things in life other than ballgames and auditions and arguments.

He hated seeing where Katie lived though. The stairways were dark and narrow, and the hallways were noisy and dirty. But she loved it, and he applauded her for trying as hard as she was.

When she opened her door at the end of the dark hallway he was cheered just seeing her face. She looked so happy to see him, with her dark, laughing eyes and shy smile, that he just had to smile too.

"Did you get it?" she asked as he kissed her hello.

"Yup. I got it."

"You're kidding!" she shrieked. "He got it, Tara! He got it!"

Jim smiled as Katie went running in to her roommate's room.

"Wait a minute!" he heard, and a moment later Katie came out of the dining room that served as her roommate's bedroom.

"You look like the cat that just ate the canary," he said. "What are you grinning about?"

"Oh, just your part," Katie said, grinning more.

A moment later Tara came out of her room. Jim had always found Katie's roommate pretty, but today she was just plain beautiful. She was as blond as Katie but with pale blue eyes, and taller and shapelier than his sister.

She looked prettier than usual today, but what Jim noticed more than anything else was the look in her eyes. She was looking at him as a woman looks at a man, her lips parted and her pale eyes focused very di-

rectly on his. "Hello, Jim," she sighed.
"Hi, Tara."
"Congratulations."
"Thanks."
The atmosphere in the room was suddenly thick with anticipation.
"I'll make some coffee," Katie said quickly, and she hurried out of the room.
"Do you have a cigarette?" Tara asked.
"Sure," Jim answered. He lit two and handed Tara one, and followed her as she sat down on the couch.
"I'm surprised you smoke these strong ones," Tara said. "I thought you ballplayers needed all the energy you could get."
"Oh, I've got enough."
"I'll bet you do," she said softly. Her gaze deepened. "I can just imagine." After a pause whose length he could not measure, she breathed, "Tell me about the part."
"Well, it's small, but it's really great —"
"Short and sweet?"
"Oh, more like short and nasty actually. I'm the not very likable secret lover of the star of the film, Lynda Palmer."
Tara's eyes widened. "Are you kidding?" she shrieked. "That's fantastic!"
"What's fantastic?" Katie asked, coming in with a tray of coffee and cups.

"The part he got! He plays Lynda Palmer's lover!"

"I told you my brother's no slouch. He's going to be a big star."

"Oh, he already *is!*"

"I mean a film star, not just a baseball star."

"There's no question in my mind that that's next for you," Tara said, as if she had mystical powers.

"Tara's decided to try modeling," Katie suddenly said.

"Katie! I told you not to tell anyone —"

"I just told Jim, Tar. Relax."

Tara sighed and then turned to Jim. "Do you think I have a chance?"

He laughed. "Oh, yes, Tara. I think anyone would say a resounding yes."

Tara smiled and her eyes shone. "Thanks," she said softly. "And who knows? You might play my lover someday if things go the way I plan. I'm going to do exactly what Katie told me you're doing — with a personal manager and all that. Only I'd want mine to be a man."

"Why?" Jim asked. "What if you found a woman who was really great at it?"

Tara shook her head. "Nope. It just wouldn't work. There has to be a chemistry, I think, a feeling that you'd do absolutely anything for your manager. And I couldn't feel that with a woman."

"Well, I understand that," Jim said, "but why should you feel you'd do anything? The manager is working for *you* — not the other way around."

"That's true," Tara conceded, "but it can't work, I don't think, unless you feel you've really put yourself into the manager's hands. That must be weird for you actually."

"Why?"

"Well, I'm all for women's lib and all that, but I think there are limits. I don't see how you can do what I was talking about — having a woman tell you what to do."

"I agree," Katie put in.

Jim shook his head. "I can't believe what I'm hearing. You two are eighteen years old and you're serious about what you're saying?"

"Jim, you used to be the world's biggest m.c.p.!" Katie said.

"That was a long time ago, kid. And anyway" — he winked — "I'm a man, I have the right. You're supposed to be the ones who are going to fight for your rights."

"I want my rights," Tara said. "I just

think there are certain things a woman can't do. And one of them is what your manager does."

Jim sipped his coffee and remembered the last words Andrea had said to him: *It can be broken. There are clauses.*

Lord, had she meant that?

He had been angry. Damned angry. She had come at him like . . . And suddenly he realized. She had come at him like Barbara, his last girlfriend before Claudia. Barbara had driven him crazy because she had been so possessive, so clinging. Claudia had seemed the opposite, but later he realized she had taken on a certain calculated casualness that was false, knowing that was what he wanted. And when Andrea had come at him like that, like the classic angry wife with actual photographic evidence in her hands, he had reacted.

But what had he said? That he'd never promised to spend every night with her.

He had said that to Andrea, beautiful Andrea, who had made the past couple of weeks great, who wasn't like anyone he had ever been with before.

And now she wanted out.

"Katie, let me use your phone," he said.

As Andrea slid on to the banquette in

the softly lit corner of La Fourchette, she felt as alone as she ever had in her life. Sloan had suggested they go out for a drink since it was the end of the day and she looked "miserable," and she had agreed because she couldn't find any good reason not to. But Sloan had taken her to La Fourchette, a place they always went to for celebrations, and the memory of all those good times made her present pain seem all the deeper.

The restaurant was beautiful. With its burnished pine walls and thick mahogany bar, the art deco mirrors and pristine black and white marble floors, it had always reminded Andrea of a movie set. She and Sloan knew the owner, and he had told them once that the only nonperiod objects he allowed in the restaurant were his kitchen utensils. And Andrea was pretty sure he stuck to his rule: the glasses, the silverware, the chandeliers, were all antiques and all magnificent. Yet all of it made Andrea resentful. Everyone around her seemed to be celebrating something, and she was as depressed as she had felt in months.

"I don't want to say I told you so," Sloan began once their drinks arrived.

She gave him a black look. "Then don't,

okay?" She sighed. "Look, I'm sorry, Sloan, but no one likes to hear that."

"I know, kid, but sometimes it has to be said. You walked into this thing with your eyes shut tight because you knew what you'd see if you looked at the problem."

She sipped at her Campari and soda, which at that moment seemed to be the one welcome element in the world. "Oh, come on, Sloan. What about us?"

He blinked. "What *about* us?"

"Well, would you have started the affair if you had been rational about it? Obviously not. Sex automatically complicates any situation, and there's no mystery about that; it's a given. And I can handle that part, just the way we did. Only I wonder what's going to happen to . . . to the whole relationship."

"He's called twice this afternoon," Sloan said. "When are you going to call him back?"

She sighed. "When I think he's really thought about things," she finally answered. "I know the way he works. He's realized, maybe, that he's made a mistake as far as the professional relationship goes. He got the part, and that's what's important to him now. And he has a tendency to be very opportunistic. He'll want to forget about what happened and what we both said. Only I can't forget." Her throat began to close over her voice as she remembered some of the things Jim had said. He was so angry, so nasty. That first comment he had made about not promising to be together every night had hurt more than the others. Where had that come from, and why had he assumed she even wanted that?

He was so defensive. And the rest — what he had said about needing to get out from under her: Was it true? Or had he just said that because he was angry?

It had to be true, she realized, because he hadn't called her the night before the audition; he had needed time to himself. Which was fine. Only it hinted at a future she didn't really want to look at. As Jim got more and more successful, he'd have to "get out from under" her in ways much more significant than just staying apart for one night. He already resented her role and she had barely begun her work with him; what would happen when he became really successful?

"Andrea?" Sloan said softly.

"I really don't want to talk about it anymore, Sloan, okay? I mean, it was nice of you to suggest we get out of the office and talk, but this is one I have to handle by myself."

He looked into her eyes. "All right," he said quietly. "But I want you to know that I'm ready to handle Jim if you want out of that end of it. All right? And do me a favor. Consider that as a possibility."

She sighed. "It *would* make things so much easier. But I don't want to give that up. I have a lot of plans for him."

"Then you have some serious thinking to do. Really, Andrea, I don't see it working and I can't visualize its improving."

She gazed into his eyes and wondered whether he was speaking the truth. Lately she hadn't quite trusted Sloan, and this morning he had seemed almost sly.

Did she really have to make a choice?

And worse yet, would the choice be hers to make?

Andrea left Sloan at La Fourchette and walked home. It was a time of year she loved, with the air cool and crisp and the sky, even over New York City, a deep, clear blue. And she usually enjoyed walking too. It was exactly a mile and a half between her office and her apartment, and whenever she took long walks she was usually energized by the exercise.

But today walking back from the restaurant was like waging a war. Everyone seemed to bump into Andrea, and she knew she probably looked like one of those people on the street about whom you wonder, What was bugging *them?* But she walked on, knowing that physical activity was the only way she was going to be able to release some of her tension.

She was still wound up when she got to her building. When the elevator didn't come she almost kicked the doors and when it finally did arrive and a neighbor said a jaunty "Good evening," she muttered an unintelligible reply and let the door slam shut.

She felt simply wretched. She wished she could stop thinking about Jim and turn her thoughts elsewhere — even to other problems she had at work. But she couldn't.

The elevator door opened and she stepped out into the hallway, having decided on one thing: she would take the phone off the hook, take a bath, curl up with a good book, and force herself not to think about Jim.

But when she fished her keys out of her purse and looked up, she saw Jim standing at the end of the hall.

"Jim!"

"I had to see you," he said, coming forward. "Why didn't you call me back?"

She walked past him and opened her door. "I thought we both needed time to think."

As he followed her in she was annoyingly aware of his closeness, of the musky scent that made her remember roving her lips across his chest, taking his nipples in her mouth, making him whisper her name with pleasure. She remembered other times when he had come in to the apartment with her, when they had both been drunk with anticipation of the lovemaking they knew was theirs for the night, when they would fall into each other's arms the moment the door closed. Only that wasn't going to happen tonight.

Maybe it wasn't going to happen ever again.

She set down her purse in the foyer, kicked off her shoes, and padded into the sunken living room to make herself a drink.

"Do I get one of those?" he called, coming down the steps.

"Sure," she said tonelessly. "What do you want?"

"A Scotch and soda," he said as he came and stood next to her. "And you."

She didn't even turn around. "Listen, Jim," she began, taking out two glasses. But she looked down and saw she had already taken two out. Damn it, she couldn't concentrate! "We really — both of us — have a lot to think about. I mean, what we had was really nice, but —"

" 'Had'?" he interrupted. He turned her around and put his hands on her shoulders. "What are you saying?" he asked softly. The tenderness in his voice was even more eloquent than the gentleness of his hands as he held her and gazed into her eyes. "Andrea, I *have* been thinking. And I'm here because I don't want you to be thinking about what I said without first hearing that I'm sorry." His eyes pleaded with her, drawing her in though she resisted. "Really. I don't know about the drinking business; I guess I was out of line there too. But I don't think that's what either of us is thinking about." He sighed. "What I'm really sorry about is what I said before — when I said I didn't want to spend all my time with you; I didn't mean it the way it sounded."

She twisted out of his grasp and poured two Scotch and sodas just to give herself time to think. He sounded so sincere, so wonderful. But wasn't it regret talking as much as anything else? Regret, and fear that she would try to end the relationship? Maybe he was saying things he didn't really mean.

She handed him his drink and they walked over to the couch and sat down. After she took a sip she said, "Look, I don't want you to get the wrong impression. I don't know where you got the idea that I was asking for that anyway."

"But I do," he said quickly, taking her hand in both of his. "And I want to tell you because there's no way you could possibly know otherwise. I realized it this afternoon when I was at Katie's house. I was acting as if you were Barbara, the woman I went out with before Claudia. She was very nervous, very possessive, really unsure of herself, and always worrying that I was cheating on her. We couldn't go to the movies without her asking if I thought the girl who sold us the tickets was prettier than she was. And then she'd be upset because the women in the movie usually *were* prettier than she was. And I didn't care — I was with her, not with them, and I knew her. But after a while it got to wear really thin. I did start looking at other women and wishing I were with them." He took a sip of his drink and kept hold of her hand with his other hand. "Anyway, I guess I snapped like that because the whole situation was too reminiscent of the Barbara thing. And I'm sorry. It was a rotten thing to say."

"But you *did* mean some of it, Jim, and that's what — that's what makes me think we should stop seeing each other." She slipped out of the warmth of his hand.

"What do you mean? That we'd stop seeing each other completely? Why? I just explained —"

She shook her head. "It's going to get too difficult, Jim. I can just feel it." She sighed. "I couldn't think straight about it this afternoon; I guess I really couldn't think straight until now. But now I know."

"Know what? I don't understand."

"I know that I want to be your manager. I want to see you get what you want, Jim, to be a really respected actor, to get the kind of recognition for acting that you had for baseball. And I know that we can't do both. We just can't have this kind of relationship and have me be your manager. It just won't work. So after your interview with Alan Crispen tomorrow, I think we should try to put things on hold."

He looked at her in astonishment. "You know, Andrea, since the first time I saw you in all those years, you started in on me for being some kind of womanizer. You mentioned that I went out with ten girls at a time, which is a little bit of an exaggeration, and I think you felt I hadn't changed. I have an image and I know that. But now you come along with this . . . this proposition which sounds damned superficial to me. If you want out, then tell me that; don't couch it in terms of some crazy idea."

"It's not a crazy idea," she objected. "And it's not forever. But it's the only way I can work with you."

"And then what?" he demanded. "When do we decide — or you decide — that we get back together? When I've gotten a part in a play? Two movie roles? It doesn't make any sense, Andrea." He sighed. "Look, I admit I felt I had to get out from under you last night. I felt as if I were in your power, or as if I suddenly wasn't supposed to do anything without your permission. But that's something I'm going to work on, or that we can work on together. If we pretend it isn't there, Andrea, it's just going to be a hundred times worse when we finally do get together. We won't have faced it, and it'll just have grown."

She hesitated. What he was saying made

sense. And he was talking as if he really cared, as if he really wanted to try to work on the problems he knew would crop up in their relationship. And she loved that. One of the reasons she had broken up with several of the men she had dated in the past few years was that they were never willing to work on any problems or questions or uncertainties in the relationship. One of them had even said to her, "That's such a woman's magazine term: to 'work on' a relationship. Why would something good need work?"

And here was the man she loved — the last person in the world she would have expected to hear those words from — saying he wanted to work on something. She loved it.

"I love what you're saying, Jim, but how are we going to take care of it? I don't want you resenting me all the time."

"I won't resent you," he murmured, pulling her up so they were both standing, gazing into each other's eyes. "I can't for too long when I know we can make love and make everything perfect again." As he brought his hands to the small of her back and held her against him, the heat that burned the minute she came near to Jim began to simmer in her veins. "And there's something you have to understand," he said huskily as he began leading her to the bedroom.

"What?" she asked softly, walking in time with him. Already their bodies were adjusting again, getting into perfect tune and rhythm with each other.

"I'm not going to let anything more interfere with us from now on. It could be you or me or someone we hardly know, but whoever and whatever tries to break us apart, Andrea, watch out. Because I'm never — ever — going to give up making love with you."

By the soft light of the moon slanting through her window, Andrea gazed up with joy at the man she loved as he held her in his arms.

"Now, just tell me something," he murmured, his lips grazing her cheeks, her lips, her neck. "Do you think I'm going to let you go?"

She smiled. "I don't know."

"The hell you don't," he said hoarsely. He took her face in his hands and kissed her long and hard, deep with passion and the need he had been holding back, his tongue suggestively teasing and coaxing her own.

He tore his mouth away, and with a

moan covered her lips again as his hands moved over her waist and the curve of her hips, as they grasped her buttocks and held her close.

"You think I'm going to give you up?" he asked, planting wet kisses along her neck. He unbuttoned her shirt and slid it off, then unhooked her bra and gazed at her. Just watching him as he took such obvious pleasure in her breasts made her want him, and it made her think about how different he was from other men. He took pleasure in her pleasure and in every part of her body, and he seemed to love taking his time in a deliciously lingering way.

He lowered himself and took a nipple into his mouth, bringing it to a fiery peak as he played with the other between his fingers.

"Darling," he whispered as he kissed the other tender bud, cupping her breast in his warm hands. He trailed his fingers to her waist and unzipped her skirt, and moments later he laid her back on the bed, freed of all her clothes.

He looked down at her in wonder, more amazed by her perfection than ever. Just looking at her was incredibly arousing, heating him with a demanding need that cried out to be satisfied. But with Andrea he liked to draw out their pleasure, to enjoy what he had never enjoyed so much with any other woman — her breathless responsiveness, her cries of joy, her hoarse whisperings of love. She always wanted to go more quickly than he did, urging him to come to her, capturing his pleasure with coaxing fingers that dared him to hold back. But each time he forced himself to wait, holding back until Andrea was awash with need and at the brink. And then he'd give in, searing himself with flaming pleasure as he entered her.

Now, as his need grew just at the sight of her, he began pulling off his clothes.

Andrea rose to help him, but he eased her back onto the bed.

"Let me help," she insisted.

He winked. "Nah. You're too slow."

"Oh, sure! I know what it really is, you narcissist! Mr. April! You want to show off, don't you?"

"You mean my gorgeous body?" he teased.

"Yes," she said, smiling. "You never have gotten over that centerfold experience, have you? All those hot letters from your so-called readers. You'd probably like to get cast in a movie about a male stripper, now that I think of it."

He grinned. "That's not a bad idea at all." He slid his belt out of his pants and laughed as he gave it a perfunctory wave over his head. "There. Do I have the touch?"

"Not *that* touch," she laughed. "You're supposed to entice me. To tease me, Jim, not act as if you're undressing at Brooks Brothers." Actually she wasn't quite telling the truth. Anything Jim did was mesmerizing. With his bare chest and snug-fitting jeans, all he had to do was stand there and he exuded sexuality, desire, animal need.

"All right, how's this?" he asked. He turned around and walked over to her clock radio, which he put on and turned to a rock station, and then, with a grin, tentatively at first and then with more sureness, began to deliver a very funny and very accurate imitation of the male strippers Andrea had seen on cable TV. Just barely succeeding in fighting a smile, he kept his mocking, heavy-lidded gaze on Andrea as he pranced and bumped, ground and thrust in front of her. In classic strippers' tradition, his fingers teased at the opening of his pants as he strutted and gyrated, and Andrea smiled, but when he slid his pants down and off, Andrea was filled with desire as he continued the dance. He was so perfectly built, so magnificently proportioned. And he so clearly wanted her.

He stepped on his belt buckle and let out a stream of curses. Andrea laughed and held her arms out. "Come here, you nut," she teased.

And he obliged quickly, tearing off his briefs and stretching out on the bed beside her.

"Darling," he whispered.

She smiled. "You really are a nut, you know."

He feigned concern. "Was that too silly to be sexy?"

"It was silly because you can't keep a straight face," she murmured, sinking her lips into his neck. "But it was very, very sexy too."

Her tongue traced a line down to his chest and found the hardness of one of his nipples, and she let a hand rove further, down the ripples of his chest, over his ribs, over the flat of his stomach and down.

"Andrea," he whispered. "Oh, yes, darling."

With her lips and tongue she brought each nipple to a peak and then burned a path down his stomach, following the line of hair at the center down to his aroused male strength.

"Andrea," he cried hoarsely, caressing her hair with his fingers. "Darling Andrea," he whispered as she let her magic weave its spell over him.

"Come to me," he urged, and she rose up and he laid her back on the satin softness of the bed, moving over her.

"Now you see," he said softly, gazing into her eyes. "Now you see why I can't give you up, why it would be crazy for us to be apart."

She could feel the strength of his desire between her legs, the racing of his heart against her chest as he spoke.

"I could never be around you without wanting you. I can joke around and strip and laugh, but I want you more than I've ever wanted any woman in my life."

"Then take me," she whispered. "Show me, Jim." He took a deep breath, his nostrils flaring, and moved a warm hand between her thighs, causing her to tremble with pleasure. "Jim," she whispered.

"Tell me you'll never leave me," he urged huskily.

"I won't," she whispered. "I won't leave you."

"I want you always," he rasped. And then he made them one, bringing them together with thrilling force that made

Andrea cry out. She grasped at him and moaned as he claimed her mouth with his, as his strokes brought her ever closer to blazing bliss. Though he had been joking around only minutes ago, tonight their lovemaking was serious, reaching her in ways it never had before. And when she crossed the brink, dissolving in rapture, he followed right after, gasping with pleasure at release.

And when he held her in his arms a few moments later and gently stroked her hair, whispering quiet words of affection, she almost, but not quite, felt secure about their relationship. She knew that the longer she stayed awake, the more the uncertainties would begin to plague her once again. During lovemaking was the only time she didn't feel this way. And she wanted to keep the mood, to try to feel as she had only moments ago.

"By the way," she murmured, lazily running a hand along his chest.

"Mmm?"

"You won your bet; you *are* my favorite client."

He smiled, but in his eyes she saw a mysterious sadness.

CHAPTER SEVEN

When Andrea awakened she was in Jim's arms, enveloped by his warmth and his love. In those first moments of awakening she felt truly loved as she remembered their love-making of the night before. Yet, as she grew more wide awake, she grew more fearful as well. It was all too good in some ways. When she had in essence threatened Jim last night he had become the model lover, promising to help try to work their problems through and acting as different as he could be from her old image of what he was like. And he had told her how much he cared for her.

Yet that was as far as he had gone. Physically he had loved her deeply and passionately; but did he really love her? And which was the real Jim? The one who had made promises last night, or the one who felt that 99 percent of the men on this earth belonged with more than one woman?

She had been cheated so many times. She had been hurt, even though she had sworn she wouldn't let herself be hurt again. Relationships had never ended in anything but pain — except with Sloan. But he was the rare exception, and she suspected she had held back with him, that out of a deep and fierce instinct for self-protection an inner part of her had said, Go slowly with this one. This is your job and you don't want to lose it if things don't work out. And with Sloan, too, she had known he was basically off-limits. He was definitely — or as definitely as anyone can be — a confirmed bachelor now, seeing "no reason in the world," as he put it, ever to marry again. Whether because of this or for another reason she had never discovered, she had held back with him. But in all her other relationships the endings had been deeply and keenly painful. Even when she was the one to initiate the end. How painful it was to hurt someone else! The hurting was inevitable yet unforeseeable at the same time — for at the beginning of a relationship she naturally never envisioned the end or who would hurt whom more.

Yet now she couldn't help but feel a chilling fear as she looked at Jim and realized how much she loved him. Would she hurt one day as much as she loved him? Would the pain be as deep as her love? Or would she be proven wrong? Would Jim make the seemingly inevitable suddenly false?

Deep in her heart she knew there had to be hope. Otherwise she couldn't love him as much as she did. Yet the fear still lurked.

She reached out and gently ran her fingers through his hair and then softly touched her lips to one eyelid and then to the other. His skin was warm and he smelled wonderful and familiar. He opened his eyes and smiled and drew her into his arms without a word.

And this time their lovemaking was sweet and tender, wordless yet made up of deep meaning. Andrea felt completely loved in his arms, cherished as she never had been before. And when they came together in magical harmony their cries echoed what Andrea fervently hoped was true: they loved each other as neither had ever loved before.

When she looked into his eyes he smiled. "Now I've really got something to smile about," he said softly.

She smiled and kissed him and snuggled back down on his chest as he wrapped his arms around her once more.

"I've got to go in to work," she murmured, already drifting off to sleep again. He had taken all the tension right out of her. Nothing really seemed to matter at that moment except the warmth of his arms around her back, the soft scratchiness of his chest hair against her cheek, the gentle pressure of his chin against the top of her head. And his scent enveloping her, reminding her that they had been one and they would be one again.

"Do you really have to go?" he asked softly.

"Mmm. I've got a ten o'clock appointment," she said sleepily, "but I wanted to get in early."

"Can I change your mind?" he murmured, sliding his hands over the curve of her hips to her buttocks.

"Please." She opened her eyes then, realizing she really did have to get out of bed. "No, don't," she said gently. "I really can't."

"Will I see you later?"

"Sure. Tonight. But you can sleep late here if you want and go to that interview from here."

He stretched, his magnificent body shifting beneath hers like a lion's as he stretched his powerful arms above him. Then he relaxed and enveloped her again.

"Well, I'd rather sleep late with you than without you, but thanks. That sounds nice."

And it was a nice feeling for Andrea to get ready for work with Jim there. He teased her constantly as she dressed, but she loved it.

"You're wearing that?" he cried as she pulled a lilac silk dress out of the closet.

"Yes, why? What's wrong?"

He smiled and said nothing.

"Jim, tell me!"

"Not unless you come here."

She rolled her eyes. "Come on. I'm in a hurry."

"Then you won't find out."

She came over to the bed. "Okay. Tell me now."

He grabbed her and pulled her on top of him and whispered, "You can see right through it."

"What!"

He nodded, his eyes sparkling. "Scout's honor, Andrea."

She frowned. "Have you seen it on me, really?"

"You bet. That day when I first came to your office."

"You're right," she said, surprised. "Is it really see-through?"

He grinned. "No, silly. I just wanted to get you over here again." His hands came around her waist and pinned her firmly against his body. "Now try to go to work."

She laughed. "You wouldn't dare keep me here."

"Why not?"

"Because Alan Crispen is calling me at the office this morning. He said he wanted to ask me a few more questions before he met you. And he can't ask me if you hold me prisoner here."

"Well, in that case —" He let her go and grinned. "Be my guest and run to the office."

Andrea laughed and continued dressing. Jim teased her at every step but finally let her go, and she left the apartment feeling absolutely wonderful. She felt they had really cleared the air the night before; better yet, they seemed to get along well in small ways as well as big. And for the first time she felt the relationship had a real chance of lasting.

Soon after she got to the office, though, bad news hit. Jill McCall, Owen Fielding's secretary, called Andrea.

"I've been trying to reach Jim everywhere," she complained. "Where is he?"

"I don't know," Andrea lied. It was one thing for Sloan to know of the affair, another for a total stranger — and apparently a talkative one — to know. "I'm sure I'll talk to him this morning though. What's up?"

Jill sighed. "The worst. Owen filed papers for the lawsuit today." She paused. "He's suing Jim for ten million dollars."

"What?"

"Yup. That's for actual and punitive damages, according to the papers. Anyway, Owen didn't have me type them — that's all being done at his lawyer's office — so I really don't know the specifics. But you and Sloan wanted me to let you know when it was definite. I just wish I could reach Jim."

"Well, I'll tell him."

"I know. It's just . . . I wish I could have told him myself. Oh, well, he knows where to reach me, so just tell him I said hi in addition to the bad news."

"I will. And thanks, Jill."

Andrea hung up. Ten million dollars! Was the man crazy? Jim was very well off financially because of his baseball career, but he didn't have that kind of money.

She called Sloan and their lawyer, and then dialed her number at home. She wanted to tell Jim before he heard the news from someone else; it was the kind of story that an alert courthouse reporter would pick up and spread all over town by noon. The phone at her apartment rang, her answering-machine tape went on, and she said, "Jim? If you're there pick up, okay?" She waited. Nothing. Then she called his house; maybe he had gone home after all. Nothing. She tried her house again; maybe he had been in the bathroom. Nothing. Where was he?

Jim got out of bed and threw his clothes on. He couldn't stand to listen to that phone ring anymore. Who would be calling Andrea in the middle of the day like that, and why?

He knew he could turn up the volume on the answering machine; he had the exact same model at home. But he couldn't do it; he was afraid of hearing another man's voice.

For the first time in his life he was jealous, suspicious, mistrustful. When he had watched her get dressed this morning it was with an aching inside that came from uncertainty. He watched her slink that lacy black underwear on and he wondered why she had to wear anything that pretty if she was just going to work. He watched her slide her stockings on, spray perfume on her body, and pull on a dress that he wished she'd wear only around him. He watched her put on all kinds of makeup — eye makeup, lipstick, mascara. And that awful, mysterious ache inside of him turned to dull, all-consuming mistrust.

And another mysterious thing became clear. When he had left Andrea that first day at her office and he had felt so rotten, as if everything had turned to mud, he didn't know why he felt that way. He had loved being with Andrea and then bang! — everything had changed. Now he knew what it was. It wasn't exactly jealousy, and it wasn't exactly competitiveness, and he wasn't even sure there was a name for it until he realized what it was — inadequacy. From the time he had seen Andrea with Sloan and known the two of them were going to be partly responsible for his success or failure, he had felt vaguely left out. They were two people who knew how to do something he didn't know how to do, and they'd be doing it together. And now he realized for the first time that she had a life outside of the one she spent with him, and it was a hell of a life. To her he was a client. One of many. And, sure, he couldn't pretend she didn't care for him; he knew she did. But he was in a position he didn't like. Andrea and Sloan knew more than he did about his career, and she had just left for another day filled with activities that didn't include him. She would make plans for him, of course, and talk about him, but she would do this for her other clients, and she had an understanding of the business — with Sloan — that he simply lacked.

Jim walked over to the bedroom window, where Andrea had a bunch of photographs framed and set up on a dressing table. There was one of her laughing, pulling a white and brown dog on a leash near someone's pool. There was a crowd in the background, around a barbecue grill, but Andrea was set apart. *Probably taken by her boyfriend,* he thought. *Who else would she have smiled at like that?*

Then there was another one, of Andrea lying in a field of daisies, looking very serious and very beautiful. Jim swallowed and stared at the picture. This one there was no question about at all — it was as romantic as a picture could get. The same boyfriend maybe. Or another.

The ache inside grew worse as he realized there were millions of things he didn't know about her. Whom had she loved in her life? Whom had she hated? How did she feel now about the men she had loved?

Did she love anyone now?

Only a few weeks ago he had been going out with Claudia. He hadn't loved her; he hadn't come close to loving her. And before that there had been Barbara. Before that Angelica, Christina, Linda, Jacquie, endless numbers of girls he had liked but had never loved. He had stayed friends with a very few after they had broken up. But with most — what did he know of them now?

Would that happen one day soon with Andrea?

Jim left her apartment as quickly as he could. It had been filled with Andrea, filled with perfume and pictures and clothes and flowers and books that all told him his feelings were growing too deep too fast, that he was involved in something he could no longer control. She was a strong and beautiful and desirable woman. He could laugh and fight and make love with her all in one night — night after night after night.

He had never felt this way before; he wasn't cut out for anything this deep, this wonderful, and already he was feeling an ache that told him Andrea wasn't going to be his much longer, if she even was now.

He went back to his apartment, where there was a message from Jill and a message from Andrea. Urgent, she said.

With dread he dialed, and he was put through immediately.

"Jim, hi," she said. "I have some bad news."

He didn't say anything.

"Jim?"

"What is it?"

"Owen filed papers this morning. Jill called and had tried to get you, and she finally called us here at the office. It's pretty bad — outrageous, actually —"

"How much?"

She paused, but she finally said, "Ten million dollars."

"What!"

"I know it sounds ridiculous, but that's what he's filed for."

"I don't have that kind of money. Where am I going to get that kind of money?"

"You're not going to have to, obviously, because he's not going to win, Jim. Anyway, I'd like you to come in after your interview with Alan Crispen. Charles Danforth from our law firm will be here, and Sloan and me, of course, so —"

"Right after the interview?"

"Yes, at four. And actually I'm glad I caught you, because I want to go over what you'll want to say to Alan Crispen about the suit during the interview."

"About the suit? He knows?"

"I'm sure he does. *Faces* has good reporters and they're always writing about stuff like this."

"Great. He knows and you know and Sloan knows and Jill knows. So I'm the last to know, and now you're going to tell me what I want to say about the lawsuit."

"What?"

"Don't you think that's just a little bit ridiculous? I just found out about the damn thing; now I have to discuss it with this stranger and you're going to put words in my mouth."

"Jim, we've been over this before. You have a tendency to be, well, maybe a little too honest at times. Just a little too forthcoming. For legal purposes, if for no other reason, it's very, very important that you say certain things and that you don't say other things."

"What do you think I'm going to do, Andrea? Tell him that Owen has a good case?"

"No, obviously not." She sighed. "What's the matter, Jim?"

"What's the matter? Aren't I allowed to be a little testy when I get hit with a ten-million-dollar lawsuit? It doesn't happen every day, you know."

"But that's not what's bothering you. You don't even seem that concerned about the lawsuit. You're much angrier at me and I'd like to know why."

"Look, I don't want to talk about it, all right? What time is that lawyer coming in to the office?"

"Four, I told you. Now tell me —"

"I'll see you at four," he said, and hung up.

An hour later he sat at the Russian Tea Room in a booth across from a man who had obviously harbored a deep dislike for him before he had ever even met him. Alan Crispen was a large, lanky blond who had, when Jim arrived at the booth with the maitre d', looked him up and down as if he weren't at all what he had ordered. His handshake had been slack and dishonest, and his first question was, "So what makes you think you can act?"

The question had seemed hostile and strange to Jim, since Crispen was the one who had requested the interview, and since Andrea hadn't given him the impression he'd have to be that much on the defensive. But he answered as well as he could, telling Crispen what he had told Andrea about how acting gave him the same thrill that baseball did.

"That explains why you want to act," Crispen said. "Not why you think you can do it."

"That's something we'll just have to see when I really start performing," Jim said, but he felt he sounded weak and uncertain. He knew he could do it and he knew he was good. But he didn't want to come off sounding like a conceited monster. Now, though, he sounded just plain weak. Damn it, he didn't like these interviews at all anymore now that Andrea had shown him how reporters could twist his words out of context. And for some reason he resented Andrea more than ever as the interview continued.

"I suppose it's mostly beer commercials and baseball movies you're going to be in," Crispen said next. "That will be rather frustrating to you, I imagine."

"I wouldn't know actually," Jim offered. "My first part will be in the new Eva and Alexander Kropotkin movie. I'll be playing Lynda Palmer's lover."

"Oh, that," Crispen said. "I've heard

about the movie. I didn't hear anyone say anything about a lover though. Must be a small part."

"Small but good," Jim said.

Crispen smiled derisively. "Amazing how willingly new actors accept rotten roles just because they have no choice."

"This isn't a rotten role," Jim objected. "It's an excellent chance, and —"

Crispen waved a thin hand. "Save the fan-magazine gushing for your next interview, Jim. You don't have to pretend with me."

"I'm not pretending. It's a damned good role."

"All right. If you say so," Crispen said, shrugging. "It's not important anyway."

Jim set his palms on the table and looked Crispen in the eye. "Look, Crispen, I don't know if I'm supposed to take this crap because you write for *Faces*, but I'm not going to do it. And I don't know what your beef with me is, but you seem to have one. So why don't you tell me what it is?"

Crispen stared at him with pale blue glassy eyes. "My — you *are* a sensitive one, aren't you?"

Jim stood up. "Yeah, Crispen, I'm damned sensitive about reporters who come to me with a lot of bull about me that comes out of nowhere and that they're going to print in their magazines. I'll tell you what, though: you print whatever you want about me; I won't read that trash anyway."

He turned and pushed his way past a waiter, and walked out into the crisp October air.

An hour and a half later, at four on the dot, he walked into Hammond/Sutton and asked for Andrea. He had spent the past hour and a half walking and blowing off steam because he needed to and because he didn't want to arrive at Andrea's office and find that she wasn't ready to see him. He was too angry to deal with that.

The walking had helped. He was calm enough to talk now, to deal rationally with the lawyer and Sloan and, most importantly, Andrea. At least he hoped he was.

When he arrived he found that the lawyer was already there, and that he and Sloan and Andrea had been in conference for the past half hour. This irked him. If they had to meet to discuss his case, why hadn't he been asked? But when he was shown in to the conference room by Andrea's secretary, he held his feelings in check. What he had to say to Andrea he'd say in private.

She looked beautiful. She was sitting at the end of the table wearing the outfit he had teased her about, and even though he had thought about how beautiful she was when he had looked at the pictures of her this morning, he was astonished now by her loveliness. Her dark eyes, her lips, her whole manner was mesmerizing, and she seemed to hold all three men in her power as she spoke.

It was a mere matter of introductions — introducing Jim to the lawyer, Charles Danforth, and vice versa — but even so, Jim had the feeling that the other two men in the room were hanging on her every word and movement just as he was.

In her eyes he could see questions about why he had hung up so abruptly, whether he was feeling any different now, whether he was still angry at her, and why. But she was also professional enough not to let her feelings show too much. She explained to Jim that she had reviewed much of what he had told her about Owen with Charles, and that Charles would now summarize what their approach was going to be.

"We're going to get down into the dirt with this Owen character," Charles said, steepling his fingers above a scrawled-on yellow legal pad. "We're going to make his life such hell he won't know what hit him. Now, both Sloan and Andrea here are pretty good at getting down into the dirt, but we need you to —"

"What do you mean by that?" Jim interrupted.

Andrea and Sloan both turned to him, and the lawyer looked pale and astonished. "Mean by what?"

"You know what — that Andrea and Sloan are good at getting down into the dirt. I'd like to know what you mean by that."

"Jim," Andrea cut in, "all he meant —"

"I want *him* to explain himself," Jim demanded. "What did you mean?"

Charles blinked and swallowed. "I, uh, all I meant was that they've both been in the business long enough to know what hurts, Mr. Haynes."

"Then you should have said it in those words, Mr. Danforth. I don't want to hear those words used in connection with Andrea, all right?"

"All right." Danforth breathed quietly.

For the rest of the meeting Andrea was completely confused and mystified when she thought about Jim's behavior. When she had left him this morning he was all romance and affection. Then when she called him and told him about Owen he was furious with her for a reason or reasons she still didn't understand. And now he was like some sort of guard dog ready to attack Charles, watching and listening with unblinking vigilance. She just didn't understand him.

When the meeting was over and Charles and Sloan had left, Andrea closed the door and turned to Jim. "Why don't you tell me what's going on?"

He rose out of his chair and came forward. His blue eyes were dark with emotion, and when he took her hands in his, his grasp was tender, coaxing. "I was angry at you when I walked through those doors," he said softly.

"But why?"

He shook his head and sighed. "All this . . . all of the things that have been happening with my career — your calling me about the Owen thing, and then my interview." He hesitated, not wanting to tell her how badly the interview had gone. But he had to. He had to make real what he had realized when he had first set his eyes on Andrea at the beginning of the meeting: his career had nothing to do with his relationship with Andrea. "I walked out of the interview. I'll tell you why later.

That's not important right now."

She was baffled. "I don't understand," she said.

He smiled. "Well, *I* finally do. I've been looking for things, Andrea, things that are wrong with our relationship, things that are wrong with you, reasons I should be suspicious of you. I didn't understand how I could love being with you so much at one moment and then resent you one minute later. I jumped at everything I felt has gone wrong lately — the interview this afternoon, everything — because I needed that kind of thing to anchor me. Or I thought I did anyway." He squeezed her hands and gazed into her eyes. "Andrea, I love you. I've never said those words to a soul before. That might make me sound uncaring. I hope I've never been that. But I've never loved before, not the way I love you. And I realized this morning that there was so much — so much I didn't know about you. And I got jealous." He smiled. "I think I'm going to stay jealous. But at least now we'll both know why."

She smiled, trying to fight back tears of happiness. She knew how hard it was for Jim to say all he had said. If he had never told any woman that he loved her, it had to be very, very difficult to finally say it. But he seemed to really mean it. "I'm so happy," she said. "I love you too, Jim."

His eyes shone with pleasure as he took her in his arms. "Don't let me ruin this, Andrea. Promise me that."

"Why would you ruin it?"

"That's what people do, isn't it? People like me, I mean."

"Who are people like you?"

"People who have never been in love before," he said quietly, gazing into her eyes.

She smiled. *In love.* "It's not something you practice like pitching or catching, Jim. Or even like acting."

"Have you ever been in love before?" he asked softly. "Or maybe I shouldn't say before."

"Yes, you should," she murmured. "I *am* in love now, Jim — with you."

"Oh, Andrea," he whispered. And he kissed her then, a kiss that was sweeter and deeper and more tender than any they had ever shared. He held her face in his hands, and when he drew back and gazed into her eyes, he looked as if he were gazing at the most beautiful sight on earth. In his eyes Andrea felt as lovely and graceful as she had ever felt in her life, and in those few moments in which they looked at each other with joy and wonder and love she was wonderfully and deeply sure of his feelings.

When there was a knock at the door Andrea smiled and shook her head. "The real world is calling, Jim. Sorry. Come in!" she called.

Rachelle came in and said, "Andrea, I'm sorry to interrupt, but it's John Burrows and it's important. Should I switch it in here?"

"Yes, please do," Andrea said, and a moment later Jim watched and listened as she fought like a lioness for one of her clients while miraculously sounding totally calm on the surface.

"I know what you're asking," she said firmly, "and the answer is no and will continue to be no as long as Alicia is my client, which I assure you will be a long, long time. Alicia is *not* going to accept the part if Rafaela Girolata is in the picture. . . . No, that's not the old star system; it's common sense and I shouldn't have to explain it to you. . . . Look, take it or leave it. If you want Rafaela, fine, be my guest. But Alicia won't do it. . . . That's right. . . . All right, I'll talk to you tomorrow."

She hung up the phone and looked up at Jim, who had come over to the desk where she had taken the call. "Sorry, but that was an important call. Otherwise I wouldn't have taken it."

"Don't apologize. I like seeing you work." He smiled. "I just wish you were talking about me in that context."

"Someday," she assured him. "I promise you. Or I don't promise. I don't want to be like Owen, but I have a good idea it'll be true."

He took her hands in his and brought her close. "Tell me what you have to do for the rest of the day." His voice was husky, and as he held her against his lean frame, the heat coming from his body made her weak with desire. "How soon can you leave?"

She smiled. "One declaration of love and you're ready to sweep me off my feet and out of here?"

"Yes," he nearly bellowed. "I want to do this thing right. From now on it's just the best restaurants, the best —"

She laughed. "Jim, stop."

"Why? What's the matter?"

"You don't have to give me 'the best' except your best — or your real feelings whatever they are. You're not buying me. I love *you* — not what you can get me or give me or where you can take me."

"I want to take you home," he murmured hoarsely. "I want to make up for all the times I've been such a jerk. I want everything to be perfect from now on."

She smiled. It was obvious that he *hadn't* ever had a really deep relationship before, for if he had, he would have known it couldn't be perfect. But she thought it was wonderful that this man who had once said men weren't made for monogamy was now so idealistic and enthusiastic.

"Well, I'll tell you what," she said. "I have a few calls to make and then there really isn't any reason I can't leave."

He was slowly shaking his head from side to side. "Some sense of timing, Andrea! A man tells you he loves you and you want to make a few calls." He was half-smiling, but underneath she felt he was also a bit hurt.

"Give me ten minutes and I'm all yours."

"Well, that's better. I guess I can stand a ten-minute wait if I have to."

"Yes, you have to," she teased. "So follow me. You might as well wait with me in my office."

"I had no intention of letting you out of my sight, darling."

As they walked down the thickly carpeted hallway of Hammond/Sutton, Andrea marveled at how her life had taken such an unexpected turn. For a while now she had put the old Jim Haynes out of her mind: she loved the Jim Haynes she knew now — not the boy she had fantasized about from afar in high school. Yet now, as she looked at him in that context, she was amazed that real life had not only made her dreams come true but surpassed her dreams. She loved him and he loved her. What more could she ask for?

CHAPTER EIGHT

"Tell me about the interview," Andrea said as she and Jim stepped into his apartment.

He turned her around and put his arms around her. "I don't want to talk about the interview. I want to make love."

"So do I," she said placatingly — and truthfully. "But I have to know."

He let her go and walked to the bar. "There you go again," he called over his shoulder as he poured himself a drink. "Are you always this romantic?"

"Jim, come on. I just wanted to know. I won't be able to stop wondering unless you tell me."

He handed her a Campari and soda and took his own drink over to the couch. "All right," he said, sighing and leaning back. "I'll tell you. I walked out on the bastard."

"Why?"

"Because he was a sarcastic, dishonest, sleazy excuse for a reporter who was baiting me over and over again, and who did it one too many times." He sipped his drink and looked at her. "Which was one of the reasons I was mad at you, by the way. You had spent so much time coaching me for the damned thing, but you never warned me that he was a creep."

"I'm sorry," she said. "Really. I had no idea. He was so polite to me over the phone."

"Yeah, well, he must have used up his supply of politeness damned fast."

"I really am sorry, Jim."

He shrugged. "It doesn't matter anymore. I can't hold you responsible for all that stuff and you can't know everything, so forget it. It doesn't matter."

"Okay." She sighed. "Are you angry?" She reached out and touched his cheek. It was warm and rough, with contours she knew in her lips, her cheeks, her whole body. She loved him so much. "I just had to talk about the interview because I couldn't stop thinking about it, Jim. You mentioned it and then you dropped it."

He nodded slowly. "Look, we talked about it, okay? There's no point in talking about it even more."

"You *are* angry. I'm sorry."

She let her hand rove from his cheek down to his shoulder, and then she came around and kissed him on the mouth. "I love you," she whispered when she drew back.

His eyes were more intense than she had ever seen them — deep blue, dark with emotion, brimming with love.

He cupped her face in his hands. "Maybe I love you too much," he murmured, gazing at her.

"That's impossible," she whispered.

"Darling," he sighed.

Their clothes came off quickly as they undressed each other, and each time Andrea caught Jim looking at her face she smiled at the new light in his eyes, an expression that seemed to reflect his happiness over having finally told her how he felt. And when they brought their naked bodies together he showered her with kisses and held her with such tenderness and love, she wondered whether she'd ever be happier than she was at that moment. And their love was more blissful than ever as he brought her to ecstasy again and again and then joined her, deeply and rapturously, in a breathless explosion of pleasure.

"I just realized something," he said softly, inhaling the sweetness of her hair and her neck.

"What's that?" she asked, shifting so she

could look into his wonderful eyes.

"Every time I've ever been with anyone else, I've felt so lonely after making love. I've felt like I did something that's over and done with — something finite, I guess. And it's always gone stale after a while. Only with you, it just keeps getting better and better." He smiled. "And better."

"I'm so glad you feel that way," she murmured, reaching out and stroking his hair. "That just . . . makes me feel great."

"But what about you?" he asked softly. "There's so much I don't know about you. And before, when I asked you, you never told me whether you had ever loved . . . or been in love."

"Oh . . ." She hesitated. "It's so hard to say. For me anyway. I look back on relationships where I know I felt I loved the man. And I guess I did. But I can't see it now; I don't feel it; so I don't know if it was really true. And that sort of makes me sad. I know there are people whose feelings don't fade like that, and I wish . . . Well, Sloan is the only one I'm still really friends with, other than —"

"Sloan?"

"Yes, Sloan. I went out with him a little after he first hired me, and —"

"You went out with Sloan?" he repeated, sitting up.

She propped herself up so she could look at him. "Yes. It was a long time ago — five and a half years actually."

He didn't say anything. He turned away and got his cigarettes and lighter off the night table, and he lit up in silence.

"Jim?"

"I can't believe you didn't tell me that," he said quietly.

"Why? What does it matter?"

He stared at her. "What does it matter? You spend nine, ten, who knows how many hours a day with a man you used to go out with and you ask what it matters? How long did you two go out together?"

"Three months. Three and a half, I guess."

He closed his eyes.

"Jim, I can't believe you're making such a big deal out of this."

"Well, I can't help it, all right? I find it damned weird that you kept this from me until now, and —"

"I didn't 'keep it' from you. It just never came up. Really. I — we never talked about this before."

He looked into her eyes, but the gaze wasn't affectionate. It was suspicious and probing, and she felt as if she were under a microscope. "How do you feel about him now?" he demanded.

"I like him; that's what I was telling you. But that's all — there's no romance; there are no big undercurrents. What I was *going* to say was that it makes me feel good that I still know and like Sloan. I hate the idea that when two people break up they can't be friends."

He smoked his cigarette and said nothing.

"Jim, what's wrong? I really don't understand why it's that big a deal."

He sighed. "This has been one hell of a day," he said quietly. "When it rains it really pours, doesn't it?"

He swung his legs off the bed and stood up, and a moment later, clad in a black silk bathrobe, he left the room without a word.

Andrea felt awful. Jim seemed really upset. And everything she said just seemed to make him even more upset.

She leaned back against the wall and wondered what to do. If she went out and talked to him, she might make it worse. But if she didn't, what would happen?

She pulled on a shirt of his and padded out to the living room. It was dark except for one light, an arc of chrome that came up from the floor and cast a circle of light around Jim and the balcony doors. Jim was still smoking, and he didn't look up when she approached.

"Jim?"

His eyes were dark and angry.

She came out and sat on the ottoman in front of his chair. "I still don't know why you're so angry. I promise there's nothing going on between me and Sloan."

He took a deep breath and let it out slowly. "It's not really that," he said, stubbing out his cigarette. "It just . . . came at a bad time. I don't know if anyone else can really understand this, but it's very hard for me right now, to be at the beginning all over again after being on top for so long. I'm trying to get used to the fact that you know more about what should happen to me than I do; and I was just getting used to the fact that you and Sloan worked together and *do* know more than I do about certain areas. That really isn't the end of the world. But I had felt, oh, that with you, knowing you loved me and that I loved you, that I could do anything — that together we could conquer the world even though that sounds corny. And to know then that you and Sloan . . ."

"That was years ago," she insisted softly. "Really. And it wasn't that great anyway.

We're friends, but there was a lot wrong with the relationship. And what we had will definitely never happen again."

As Jim watched Andrea talk he couldn't believe how he had fallen in love so unexpectedly. Why hadn't he known he'd fall for those beautiful green eyes? Why hadn't he known he'd fall for this woman who was so wonderful in every way?

He had never loved before — not like this and not even close. A day ago he had been frightened; he knew he had let himself in for future pain that seemed inevitable. How many men had he seen who hadn't been hurt? He could think of only a few. And it had always amazed him that people thought men were so hard-hearted, that they never got hurt and never made any real emotional investment in a relationship. He knew lots of men who had been hurt badly, and maybe some of them had brought it on themselves by fooling around behind their wives' backs. What had they expected? But when those wives finally walked out, those guys hurt badly.

And as he looked at Andrea he couldn't help resenting what she had become in life — a strong and successful businesswoman — because he was sure it was that aspect of her life that would in the end destroy their relationship.

He thought of how different she had been in high school, especially that day she gave him back the story — beautiful but shy, so shy he had been charmed. If only he had gotten to know her then! He was still a hero then, still someone she could look up to.

"Jim, I wish you'd believe me."

"I do believe you — about Sloan anyway," he said quietly. "But I just feel like the guy who's lost his job or his livelihood. He comes home and he tells his wife he's been laid off, and she says it's okay and she still loves him, but he can never quite believe her now that he's been stripped of something he considers so important."

"You haven't been stripped of anything," she said softly. "And anyone would feel down after getting sued and having a rotten interview. Just wait until shooting on *The Princess of Destiny* begins. Then I *know* you'll feel better."

Three days later Jim reported to work on the set of *The Princess of Destiny*, the Plaza Hotel, where the Lynda Palmer character, Gloria Plimpton, lived whenever she was in New York rather than Paris or London or Rome. Jim had been on television hundreds of times, both during games and in interviews, but just seeing the set of *Princess* was exciting. Though much of the shooting would take place in the hotel's restaurants, the city streets, and Paris, a good portion of the movie would be filmed in a fifteenth-floor corner suite overlooking Central Park and midtown Manhattan, and this was where Jim reported to work on the first day of filming.

The suite was magnificent — it was made up of ten adjoining rooms, just the kind of place that would be suitable for a character like Gloria Plimpton. This was a woman who had married for money rather than for love, whose trial-lawyer husband was usually conveniently out of town whenever she was in town. And every detail of the suite — from the French Provincial furniture to the lace curtains to the pure linen sheets — was fit for Gloria Plimpton, the kind of woman who would demand perfection in everything money could buy.

Jim smiled as he thought of his role. Kyle Whiting would be a lot of fun to play. He played a character Gloria Plimpton couldn't buy, but not because he couldn't be bought — simply because his price was too high. He wasn't a gigolo in the strict sense of the word, but he wasn't free either. He was a young lawyer at Gloria's husband's firm, and he wanted Gloria to steer him as many prime cases as she could. What he didn't know was that she didn't have that kind of power where her husband was concerned. She was an ornament to the man, a symbol of status just as his houses and cars and prize Thoroughbreds were. She could be replaced if necessary. And Gloria knew this. But she also wanted Kyle Whiting, so she never let on that she didn't have the kind of power he thought she had.

One thing Jim liked about the part was that it was so well written that all of the machinations and conflicts — in fact, Kyle and Gloria's whole relationship — were encompassed in one scene. They met at a party, they made love after almost no conversation, and *then* they talked. Whiting expected cooperation, she said she'd see what she could do, he saw she was lying, and he walked out of her life forever. Naturally Jim wished the part were larger, but he knew it was like a small gem, much better than a lot of larger, less valuable parts he could have gotten.

As the cast and crew assembled in the large suite, Jim looked for Lynda Palmer and wondered whether she'd come later. She was the most well known of the whole group besides Jake Curtis, and he had the feeling he had read somewhere that she was chronically late.

But just then someone behind him slid an arm around his waist and said, "Hello, handsome," and he turned to find that he was looking into the lake-blue eyes of the beautiful Lynda Palmer.

Andrea had her hands full. Now that Owen had filed papers it was a sure bet he'd start having his publicity mill churn out negative rumors about Jim. He had to realize that filing suit could hurt him because potential clients would perhaps see him as a victim and wouldn't want to associate with him. She was sure he'd make it seem as if he had been unjustly wronged and that his organization was aggressive, strong, and willing to do whatever they had to in order to right this terrible wrong.

Andrea's only problem was that Jim had nothing to plug or promote at this point. These days, 99 percent of the guests on talk shows were there to show a film clip or, less frequently, to discuss their latest part in some new Broadway play. Or they sang or danced or told jokes, of course.

But if they were actors, they were there to promote.

The first thing she did was call Alan Crispen to try to find out what had gone wrong. He said he wasn't going to write the article after all because there was "nothing to write," and she told him he was obviously free to write whatever he wanted but that she wasn't going to let her clients speak with him if she knew he was always going to have a chip on his shoulder. He got annoyed, she got more annoyed, and she ended up hanging up on the man. So much for one contact at *Faces*.

There were so many things she could do if she were going to go the beefcake-ex-sports-star route. Jim could do everything from appearing in boys'-wear departments for special promotions to endorsing baseball accessories. But how was she going to get his name in the news *now*, before there was reason to?

Ten minutes later she had called three contacts at three different talk shows, and all had agreed to invite Jim on their shows. The idea that he wasn't following the usual ex-jock route was appealing to them all, and his part in the new Kropotkin movie gave an added luster; he could certainly talk about it even if he didn't have a clip.

"I hear he's a dreamboat," Claire Conley from the Bill Stephenson show said.

Andrea smiled at the old-fashioned word. "He is," she answered. "I think that's the perfect word for him."

Jim, meanwhile, was getting acquainted with Lynda Palmer. She seemed fascinated by him, which he couldn't fathom at all since Jake Curtis was in the suite along with lots of other people she presumably knew and liked.

But it was Jim she stayed next to, entwining her arm with his as they listened to the director, Art McKeon, talk.

Jim didn't want to stare at Lynda, but she was even more beautiful than she looked on screen. Her hair was a rich, dark auburn, flowing and wavy and very soft-looking; her eyes were the bluest he had ever seen, and her body — well, she was perfect, with legs that didn't quit and a tiny waist, and breasts that were high and full and unbelievably inviting in what she was wearing — a low-necked green hostess gown that must have been designed just for her.

As she stood next to Jim she moved closer, her hip insisting against his and her arm squeezing his against her body.

Oh, Lord, he thought. *Get me out of this.* He felt as if he were being put to some sort of test, as if, having declared his love for Andrea, he would now have to meet and get close to every beautiful woman in the world.

Maybe testing was a good thing, of course. He realized that seeing Tara that day had been a kind of test, too, because he had seen that while she was young and beautiful and more than willing, what he wanted was a grown woman, a woman he loved, and only one woman in the world — Andrea.

But Lynda was going to present special problems. He was going to have to do a love scene with her. And he wasn't sure she'd be acting. . . .

Over the next few days Jim watched the filming of *Princess* and spent the nights with Andrea. Andrea was very happy with the change she felt had come over him; he seemed much happier and more confident about the future of his career. He hadn't started filming his part yet, but he was enthusiastic about the director and everyone in the film, and very excited about the talk shows she had booked him on.

"This time I'll be ready," he had said.

"They can bring on Alan Crispen or talk about Owen or whatever they want, and I'll be ready for them."

Strangely enough, though, they hadn't heard a word out of Owen — not a rumor, nothing.

Charles Danforth had spoken with Owen's lawyer and gotten nowhere, but at least Owen wasn't blanketing the city with self-protective rumors as Andrea had imagined.

And her relationship with Jim just kept improving. Andrea trusted him now, and she was grateful she had allowed herself to fall in love with him rather than say no because she was afraid; her fears about Jim's womanizing ways had proved totally unfounded.

As days went by and Jim began running through his part with Lynda, he grew close-mouthed about his part and his days on the set, but Andrea didn't say anything. She knew this was an area in which he functioned better by himself than with constant discussion, and that was his right. She remembered how after his audition for the part he had complained that everyone he had spoken to lately could talk about nothing but auditions and callbacks. And although he was skipping his group classes with Olga Rafelson for the moment while shooting was going on, she knew what he meant — he needed his independence.

Andrea, meanwhile, was very involved with a new client, a young ex-model named Lorenzo Corlezza. He was a young Adonis, dark and classically handsome, with a body that had posed in ads for everything from discount underwear to the latest designer suits. He had just landed a role in a new daytime soap, and he was ready to hit the public in a big way. The soap-opera market was a tremendous and pleasant one to tap, with seemingly endless numbers of fan magazines and new ones coming out almost daily. And a friend of hers, a young producer named Jack McKenzie, was ready to include Lorenzo in an all-soap-star special week of *Celebrity Sizzlers*, the hit quiz show. Lorenzo's female co-star, Lisbeth Casey, who played his girlfriend on the show, was rumored to be romantically linked with him off the show as well, and while this wasn't in fact true, Andrea did nothing to discourage the rumors. Lorenzo and Lisbeth would look great on magazine covers together.

The day before Jim was scheduled to start shooting his part in *Princess*, he showed up at Andrea's office unannounced.

She was just in the middle of a meeting with Lorenzo, and she told Rachelle to tell Jim she'd be with him as soon as she could.

Jim was annoyed but he also understood. He had taken a chance and come over to her office with a little surprise because they had shut down early on *Princess*, and he knew she was always busy. But as the minutes passed and he read one *People* magazine after another, he grew impatient. Was she coming out or wasn't she?

He sprang out of his chair and strode up to the receptionist. "Uh, could you tell Andrea that I have to leave?"

"Certainly, Mr. Haynes," she said softly. "One moment, please."

She never took her eyes off Jim as she pushed Andrea's extension and spoke to Andrea, and he sensed it wasn't because of the way he looked or his voice or his manner, but because he was a client of Hammond/Sutton's and he was on the way up. It was an odd feeling.

"She'll be right out," the receptionist said, and a moment later Andrea did indeed come out, but she was out of breath and obviously harried.

"Sorry," she apologized as she led Jim back into the inner sanctum of offices. "I really lost track of the time in there."

"You don't have to apologize. I just wanted to surprise you." He reached into his pocket and pulled out a small blue velvet box.

"What's this?" she asked.

He smiled. "Don't you know what day this is?"

She looked panic stricken. "Oh, no, what?"

He laughed. "Well, I guess your memory isn't as great as I thought. It's been thirty-seven days since we started seeing each other."

"Oh, Jim."

"Open it. I got it the other day after I saw you looking at it at Tiffany's."

She lifted the cover up and couldn't say a word. He had bought her the pendant she had loved, something she hadn't even thought he'd noticed. And he had gone all the way back and gotten it for her. It was a gold teardrop with an amethyst at the bottom of it, and when she had first spotted it in the store, she'd thought it was one of the most graceful pieces of jewelry she had ever seen. But now — now that Jim had gone out and bought it for her — she loved it even more.

"Jim, it's beautiful."

His eyes shone as he took her in his arms. "Not as beautiful as you. I was hoping you'd look just as happy as you look, so I'm satisfied."

"Good. I love it. Now, come on in and meet Lorenzo. I'm just finishing up with him and then we can leave together."

"Great." He followed her down the hall, and he was just basking in the afterglow of having given her something she obviously loved, when he stepped into her office and set eyes on her new client.

He was the man she had mentioned so many times over the past few weeks that his curiosity had been piqued, but he had been so wrapped up in his own life that he hadn't paid all that much attention to what she was saying.

Now he wished he had. Lorenzo was clearly competition.

And when Lorenzo looked up from what he was reading, he shot Jim a cool and aggressive stare that to Jim meant only one thing — war.

CHAPTER NINE

As Jim shook hands with Lorenzo he had the distinct impression that Lorenzo knew he and Andrea were lovers, and that he was going to do his best to take Jim's place.

"Andrea and I were just looking at the tearsheets of my latest magazine piece," Lorenzo said as he sauntered over to Andrea's desk as if it were his. "These might interest you," he added, handing them to Jim. "Since I understand you're trying rather vainly to break into acting."

Jim took the pictures without a word. Lorenzo Corlezza was so obviously baiting him that it seemed childish to respond in kind.

"Very nice," he said, barely glancing at them before he tossed them back to the desk.

"Hey! Careful with those!"

"They're just tearsheets," Jim responded. "Not negatives. And, hard as that may be for you to believe, I do know the difference."

Lorenzo blinked. "You still have locker-room manners, I see," he observed.

"Hey look, fella —"

"Jim!" Andrea cried. "Lorenzo! What's the matter with you two?"

Neither said a word. They just looked at each other like angry young bulls.

Andrea shook her head. "You're both going to turn into celebrities of the absolutely worst kind if you don't watch out."

"Sorry, Andy," Lorenzo said quickly. "You're absolutely right. And I do have to rush off actually."

Andy? Jim repeated silently to himself. What the hell was going on?

Lorenzo leaned over and kissed Andrea on the cheek. "I'll talk to you tomorrow, Andy. And call me if the Helena Parris thing comes through."

"I will," she said.

A moment later, after Lorenzo had gone, Andrea went over to the bar and poured herself a Perrier. "Do you want anything?" she called over her shoulder.

"Yes. I want to know why that — that sleazebomb called you Andy and why he kissed you good-bye. Does he kiss you hello too?"

When she turned around he saw that she was almost smiling. What the hell was she looking so amused about? "Yes, as a matter of fact, he does. He does that with everybody, or almost everybody. That's just the way he is."

"What is this Andy business?" Jim demanded, sitting back on her desk and crossing his arms.

She shrugged. "That's what he calls me. It's no big deal."

"It's no big deal. Sure. What else does he do that's no big deal?"

"Jim! Come on! You sound like a character straight out of some nineteen-fifties movie."

"Maybe that's the way I feel," he replied. "And maybe that isn't such a terrible way to be either. So I'm jealous. What's so terrible about that?"

She smiled. He looked so handsome when he was angry. And she was flattered, too, over the way he felt. But she knew it couldn't be any fun for him. "Look, I'm flattered that you think Lorenzo could be interested in —"

"Why?" he cut in. "Is he better than me? Is he such a goddamned prize that that's so flattering? You know, Andrea, there's something about this business you're in that I don't like: Why is it that every time I turn around, you're involved or almost involved or you used to be involved with every guy I meet? I don't like it!" He reached down for Lorenzo's tearsheets and held them up. "This hunk business — you told me it was no good. And here, look at this." Underneath the tearsheets were more pictures of Lorenzo, clad in what Jim could describe only as a loincloth. "Here, what the hell is this?" he demanded. "Beefcake is out! That's what you told me. And here's this guy dressed in practically nothing."

"Lorenzo is a model!" she yelled. "Lorenzo wants *entirely* different things out of his career from what you want. Entirely different. And I won't stand here, Jim, and listen to you imply that something funny goes on in this office. That's damned insulting."

"I don't want to insult you; I don't mean it the way you think, Andrea. I'm not talking about something organized, but I *am* talking about you! Every guy who walks through these doors has to want you — every guy, Andrea. They're around you, they listen to how much you know, and they admire you for that, they like you and they *have* to be attracted to you. And I don't like that because I know what happened with us and I refuse to see it happening with someone like Lorenzo. Or anyone else, Andrea. *Anyone* else."

"But it isn't happening," she said calmly, putting down her drink and stepping forward. She put her arms around his neck and looked into his magnificent eyes. "No one has eyes like yours, Jim. No one makes love to me the way you do. And I love one person right now — you."

"I wish I could be sure."

"This is as sure as anything can be, Jim, anything on this earth."

He wrapped her in his arms and rested his chin on her head. God, how he wished he could be sure.

The next day shooting on Jim and Lynda's love scene was set to begin. They had run through everything but the actual love scene, since Lynda had a policy of never rehearsing that type of scene. "I want it to be spontaneous," she was always saying. And while the decision was really up to Art McKeon, he had gone along with Lynda's wishes. He had worked with her before and knew that she knew her limits and strengths, so it was all right with him if she wanted to be fresh for the cameras.

Jim, though, was as nervous as could be. Lynda had been coming on to him more and more every day, and this morning she had slung an arm around him and breathed, "I've been looking forward to our scene for days, Jim."

Usually he found such forwardness to be a turnoff. He knew it was old-fashioned to feel this way, but he just couldn't help it. Once a relationship got started, it was different; but if you hardly knew each other, he just didn't like it.

Lynda was an exception though. She was so physically perfect in every way that it just knocked him out. Not that he would ever trade Andrea for her — ever. He loved Andrea deeply. But he couldn't help fantasizing. . . .

And today he was supposed to kiss and caress Lynda Palmer and finally take her to bed. And he hadn't asked a soul how much was supposed to be fake and how much supposed to be real.

He knew he could have asked Andrea. But these days he was asking her as little as possible and trying as hard as he could to be the best there was in the profession, to be as independent as possible. And Art McKeon hadn't said a word — maybe because he felt Jim knew the answer, or maybe because it was up to the actors. Whatever the reason, though, no one had given him a clue.

He went up to Jake Curtis — a man who was as famous as any man in America — and sat down next to him on the couch. Curtis was a mystery-novel fanatic, and he read in every spare moment, talking to almost no one.

"Uh, Jake, do you have a second?"

He put his book down and smiled. "Sure, what's up?"

"I, uh, have a question about the love scene," Jim said.

Jake grinned. "Ah. The famous question everybody's too embarrassed to ask because they think they'll sound like prudes. Everyone asks, Jim, and the answer, if you're asking about kissing, is that you'd better ask Lynda." He shrugged. "It's up to the actors. If they're involved, then naturally. Otherwise . . ." He shrugged again. "I've gotten kneed once or twice because I had the wrong idea, but with Lynda, well, you'd better talk to her about it. And the rest, kid, sorry to tell you, has got to be faked. This is an R-rated movie."

"Yeah, right," Jim said. Well, Jake hadn't been much help, but he'd find out soon enough.

A few moments later he was called to makeup and wardrobe and then he and

Lynda were at the entrance to the sitting room of the suite with cameras rolling. The moment of truth had arrived.

"I want you," she whispered, draping her arms around his neck.

He smiled — the slow, evil smile that was supposed to be Kyle Whiting's trademark — and then lowered his lips to hers.

Instantly her lips parted, and with a moan she brought her tongue to his, teasing his into her mouth and bringing him so close he could feel every curve, every heated inch of her body.

She drew back, her eyes dark with desire, and breathed, "Take me. Take me, Kyle," and closed her mouth over his again in a kiss that was shockingly arousing. Jim was vaguely aware in the back of his mind that the kiss was going on far longer than the script had indicated. But he was only vaguely aware of this.

As if reading his mind, Lynda drew back and led him into the bedroom, the cameras following, where she quickly pulled off his jacket, ripped out the knot in his tie, and let her fingers fly over the buttons of his shirt. When she parted the fabric she lowered her lips to his chest with a deep moan. When her lips found his nipple, his hands reached for the softness of her hair, and he was lost in pleasure.

As she stripped him of his shirt, his shoes, and his socks, he was aware only of the agonizingly long time it was taking and of the deep pleasure she was giving him at the same time, running her lips over each area of skin that was exposed. Only dimly he heard the cameras rolling, and once someone made a sound he couldn't identify. His eyes were closed, his hands were in her hair as she knelt before him, and when her lips roved down the center of his stomach and her hands clasped at his belt, he grew so aroused he didn't know what to do, unless he wanted to show the whole crew how much he wanted this woman.

He opened his eyes and looked down at Lynda, and she looked up at him. And in those blue eyes he saw triumph. And his desire disappeared.

"Darling," she whispered. She had covered the change, one he hoped was noticeable only to her, and her whispered urging had held a special meaning for the two of them. Then she wondered what was wrong. He sighed with relief masked as desire as he pulled her to her feet, scooped her into his arms, and laid her on the bed. She looked amazingly beautiful as she lay against the white satin bedspread, with her rich auburn hair spread in a corona around her head and her arms spread in wait for him.

But he didn't want her anymore. Thank God, he didn't want her anymore.

He stripped off his pants, climbed atop her, and Art McKeon yelled "Cut!"

Jim immediately swung off her and looked at Art McKeon.

"That was unbelievably fine," Art said. "Really beautiful work, both of you."

There were a few guffaws from the crew, and someone called out, "Yeah! Nice work if you can get it!"

Jim laughed and said, "We can do another take if we need to," but inside he was glad it was a wrap. There was something about Lynda that was uncontrollable, too seductive and unpredictable, and he was very relieved that that part of the scene was over.

During the break, as he sipped a cup of coffee by the window, he looked out at the magnificent view of Central Park and thought about what had happened. Why was he so relieved he had conquered his desire for Lynda? He felt strangely honorable, as if he had turned away from a mythical temptress.

He knew that part of the reason he had wanted so much to conquer his desire was a simple one of embarrassment — no need for the crew members to see that the centerfold hadn't lied. But the reason ran much deeper than that.

And suddenly he knew what it was. He had passed the acid test; he had come through with flying colors on a test he'd never thought he'd pass. He loved Andrea, and he desperately wanted to be faithful to her. But he hadn't trusted himself because in all the years he had dated, there had been far too many slip-ups and secret flings and rendezvous to lead him to believe he could ever be faithful to one woman.

Maybe for someone else the test wouldn't be significant, he conceded. Maybe for another man the incident would mean only that he had resisted the charms of one woman; there were millions of others who could put him to the test at any moment in the future. But he knew that for him the episode had been significant. For the first time in his life he was trying to make a relationship work, and he was beginning to succeed.

The only problem now was Andrea. Could he or could he not trust her?

With a sigh of exhaustion Andrea threw herself onto Sloan's couch and leaned her head back against the cushions.

"Oh, what a day!" she cried. "I don't know how much more of this I can take."

"Sounds good. Whenever you complain, I know business is great."

She smiled. A subtle change had once again occurred in her and Sloan's relationship. He seemed to be back to his old wonderful and trustworthy self, and she didn't know why the change had occurred but she wasn't going to question it. She suspected that he saw how good her relationship with Jim was and that he felt less compelled to be a doomsayer.

"Lorenzo is coming along beautifully," she said. "We're going to have the April cover of *Soap Opera Stars and Stories*, and Marina Heywood did a great interview with Stan Newman today. You know, the other guy at *Faces*." She stood up, went over to the bar, and poured herself a Perrier. "What are you smiling about?" she asked as she headed back for the couch.

"You. You're so transparent."

"What? Why?"

"What about bad-boy Haynes?"

"What are you talking about?"

"Rachelle told me there was a little incident in your office the other day — some kind of contretemps between Jim and Lorenzo."

"Oh, that — that was really strange. They were like wild dogs protecting their turf."

"More like angry men trying for the same woman, it sounds like to me."

Andrea made a face. "Oh, maybe. But I don't think so. Lorenzo's just Lorenzo, and Jim has been a jealous maniac lately."

Sloan nodded slowly. "That makes sense."

"Are you being sarcastic?"

"No, not at all. Come on, Andrea, don't you see? Once a guy like Jim falls for someone he falls hard and he *has* to be jealous and suspicious, because he knows how *he* used to be. It's almost impossible for him to trust."

She remembered how Jim had reacted when he heard she had once been involved with Sloan. At first he really couldn't believe that she could be uninvolved at this point, or that there was no reason for him to be suspicious. And then only the other day with Lorenzo

Corlezza — the clash between them had been immediate. And afterward Jim had railed on and on as if he had caught her making love with Lorenzo.

Maybe it was true that he couldn't trust because he had never trusted himself. Did that mean the relationship could never progress any further?

When she asked herself this question a cool ache crept into the center of her being, and she was deeply saddened. Lately she had been thinking about the future, and the kind of future her relationship with Jim could bring to her. And part of that future had involved marriage. She had imagined the little ways they'd enjoy themselves — spending Sundays in bed with the *Times*, taking long walks in the park, waking up each morning in each other's arms.

And she had imagined, at those times when she'd let her daydreams go free, that they had children. In the summers they'd go to ballgames and to the country, and in winters Jim would be right there helping her bundle up the kids to send them off to school.

She knew he had a deep sense of commitment and a real love of family, even though his own upbringing hadn't taken place in the warmest of atmospheres. But he loved his sister, and he had always gone out of his way to give her the warmth and support he felt hadn't been given by their parents. And Andrea was sure that when it came to a family of his own he would do everything in his power — *every*thing — to help everyone be as happy and feel as loved as possible.

Though she knew she was jumping the gun by letting her thoughts wander so easily into this area, she was so happy when she thought about it that she couldn't stop. So many of the men she had gone out with in the past few years had had major flaws that she felt it was almost a miracle to have found someone she thought would actually be a wonderful father to the children she eventually wanted to have as well as a wonderful husband. She remembered one man she had gone out with — a stockbroker she had met at a party. He was good for her in many ways, and there were lots of days and nights she had simply loved being with him. But underneath she had discovered a basic selfishness in him that ran very deep, and she knew then that there was no future or potential in the relationship except a future of sameness, of carrying on at the same plateau indefinitely. And she had found this to be true of many men lately.

With Jim, though, it was different. Each day he seemed to open up more and more, to be more willing to trust and love and give of himself. And she knew that inside of him there was a deep well of love just waiting to be shared.

And now what Sloan was saying was deeply disturbing. He was saying something she had sensed but never articulated before — Jim was loving and giving and sensitive, but he still had a long way to go when it came to trusting and believing in a relationship. Until now Andrea had assumed that this readiness and trust would come, and would come soon. But what if it never did? Would she be able to turn away when she saw there was no future? Would she be able to stand that?

For the next few nights Jim seemed moody and uncommunicative. He clearly had something on his mind, but trying to find out what it was was like talking to a brick wall. According to him, the movie was going well, and she knew this was true from talking to Eva Kropotkin. Something else was bothering him, but what?

After four nights of this moodiness they

were lying in bed — the only place where communication was good, where he showed her and told her how much he loved her, and she believed him. The love-making made her realize that no matter what else was wrong, their love was more important. But afterward she always felt him withdraw back into himself again.

Just when Andrea was about to say she couldn't take any more silence, Jim spoke up.

He settled himself into a pillow and gazed into her eyes. "I want to ask you something," he said softly.

She hesitated; he sounded so nervous, but she couldn't tell if he was going to ask her something bad or something good. "Okay," she said gently, but her voice sounded hollow. He had been acting so strangely after all.

"All right. What I want to ask you is whether you think this is working between us."

Her heart skipped. "This? You mean this relationship? Yes! Why? What about you?"

"I've never been . . . this involved, I guess." He thought of what had happened to him only this morning. He had gone into his exercise room to work out, and he suddenly had another picture — all the exercise equipment gone, and in its place a very different kind of room. There'd be Andrea, and him, and a child, or maybe two. And they'd make up the most loving family the world would ever know.

The thought had shocked and shaken him. He had never thought about that before. Ever.

Oh, sure, he had often sat back and thought about his life, and he had always — in the back of his mind — planned to raise a family, to give them all the love he felt had been held back in his own family. But those plans had always been abstract. They were something that would just happen to him one day, way in the future. So far in the future, in fact, that they seemed to apply to someone else, not to him. Now, though, his thoughts were very specific: he wanted Andrea to be a part of his future. Andrea and children and unending love.

He had mentioned the idea casually, cautiously, to his sister on the phone, saying he was thinking of asking Andrea to marry him.

At first Katie was silent for such a long time he wondered if she was even there. Then she had laughed and said, "Oh, you're kidding, right, Jim?"

"No, I wasn't," he had said.

"But that isn't fair," she had complained, her voice suddenly growing childish. "Tara didn't even —" She stopped.

"Tara didn't what?"

She sighed. "Well, I shouldn't be telling you this, but I guess maybe it's too late now anyway. I had planned to . . . you know . . . matchmake the two of you."

He smiled. "Me and Tara? Come on, Katie. She's a nice kid but she's a kid." *And Andrea's all woman,* he had said to himself. *The woman I want.*

Now, as he gazed into Andrea's lovely green eyes, he couldn't bring up what he had been thinking about. It would be too sudden, and it was too important. And he was afraid she'd say no.

"Are you saying we're seeing too much of each other?" Andrea asked quietly.

"Me? No, not at all. I wish we had more time together."

Andrea smiled and stretched gracefully. "Oh, one of these days I'll get lazy and take a vacation, and then maybe we can go somewhere."

"Oh, come on. I've seen the way you work; you love what you do and you probably take exactly one point seven days off every year."

"Are you crazy? Listen, I may love what I do, but I love lying on the beach even more — at least for a few days anyway. Last year I took a lot of quick trips — five days, four days, sometimes even three-day weekends someplace nice and warm. And those trips were worth every penny because I came back feeling as if I had been gone for a month. And one or two or three days off doesn't make that much difference in my office as long as Sloan is there. He can always take over."

"I never realized that," he said musingly. And suddenly he had an idea — something that would surprise her and give them both a chance to really relax.

He could hardly keep from telling her his plans. But when she wrapped her arms around him and his hands slid down to the silken skin of her buttocks, he had no trouble keeping his new plan secret. There were more important things. . . .

The next day was Jim's last on the movie. Though his scene with Lynda Palmer was long since finished, the Kropotkins had told him there was a chance they'd add another scene in which Gloria Plimpton would show up at Kyle Whiting's apartment and he'd cruelly reject her, knowing she was of no real use to him.

When he showed up, though, Art McKeon told him they had decided to follow the original script.

Jim was disappointed, but he tried to be philosophical about it. It had been a great part, and even as the part stood now, he was sure to get noticed.

As the crew was assembling and shifting furniture around, Lynda Palmer appeared at Jim's side.

"Too bad about your part," she said softly.

He shrugged. "Well, it's too bad, but I can live with it."

She leveled her blue eyes at him. "You'll go far, Jim. Don't worry; I can tell. I have an unfailing eye when it comes to future success."

He smiled. "You should be an agent. Or a manager."

She waved a dismissing hand. "Pft. Those managers. Yours is Andrea Sutton, isn't it?"

"Yes. With Hammond/Sutton."

She shook her head. "Someone should have put a stop to management teams a long time ago."

"Why? What are you talking about?"

"Oh, maybe I shouldn't really be telling you this," she began, brushing a lock of dark red hair back from her face. "I've heard you're having what someone told me was a 'torrid romance' with the woman."

"Tell me what you were going to say."

"Well, I've been around a lot longer than I look as if I have. I started in this industry when I was fifteen — modeling and doing commercials — and that's a lot more years than you've been in it, honey. And I've seen careers that could have been absolutely guaranteed just crumble to nothing."

He frowned. "Not because of managers."

"Oh, yes. Listen to me, Jim. I don't expect you to agree with me; I don't even know if you like me; but you don't have to like me in order to hear me out and give what I'm telling you some thought. Come. Let's sit down. Art is going to make us wait for the next hour anyway, so we might as well get comfortable."

They went over to a couple of gilt-edged chairs by a window and sat down.

"Now I'm going to tell you about Jayce Hartley. You know the name, right?"

"Of course," he answered.

"All right. You say 'of course.' But you don't know what that poor girl's been through lately. She was managed by Craig Heller — he's out on the coast but he has offices here in New York. Anyway, he took her on as a client — and as a lover, incidentally — and within a year you walked past any newsstand in any city and all you saw were pictures of Jayce Hartley. She couldn't do anything without success, it seemed. She acted; she endorsed face creams; she sang; they named a wine after her; she danced; she launched a line of clothes. And then something funny happened. If there had been stock in her, it would have plummeted. People got tired of the image that had been built up around Jayce because at that point it was an image with no substance behind it. Suddenly the public was sick of seeing Jayce Hartley this and Jayce Hartley that; they began to wonder why every time they turned on the TV, she was there or every time they bought a magazine, there she was on the cover. Craig Heller had saturated every medium so thoroughly with Jayce that the whole campaign ended up backfiring. She couldn't sing all that well, and she couldn't dance very well, and she could barely act. Craig Heller pushed her because she was a great beauty and he was certain she had star quality. But you know what I say? If someone has real star quality, it will come out without all that P.R. and pushing. And it will last, because it's been built on something real."

Jim shook his head. "But there are so many instances in which that hasn't happened," he objected. "Andrea and Sloan manage dozens of actors and actresses whose careers are just great. They don't push them too hard or too fast."

Lynda shrugged. "Look, for your sake, I hope I'm wrong. But let me give you one more piece of advice."

"All right," Jim said guardedly.

"Try to get your personal life straightened out so you're not involved with this woman in so many ways. I know it's none of my business, Jim, but I like you, and I'd like to see you succeed. And all I see is a road leading to a real heartbreaker of an ending."

"I don't see what the personal end has to do with it."

"You've lost your independence, that's what it has to do with it. These managers, they do everything from telling you what part to select to telling you what to wear to a goddamned benefit. You get involved with one in any deep way, and she starts telling you what brand of paper towel to buy. She'll run your life. And believe me, I've seen it happen."

"Well, that isn't the way it is with me and Andrea."

"If that's true, I'm happy for you. I really do hope it all works out for you. But I'd give it some serious thought."

"I don't have to. Andrea may tell me what to do in my professional life, but it's totally different when it comes to the two of us." He paused, wondering why he felt it was necessary to defend himself and his relationship with Andrea to someone he barely knew. But Lynda had challenged him; she had thrown doubts and questions in his face and he had to shoot them down. But suddenly all he could say was, "I know I'm right." Because he *wasn't* sure he was right; he had no answers. The issue of Andrea's career was something that had been needling him for days now — the Lorenzo business, her relationship with Sloan, the whole way she conducted herself. And unfortunately Lynda had voiced some concerns he had been holding at the back of his mind for weeks now.

But he loved Andrea. He'd go through with his plan, they'd have some time to relax, and if he felt the time was right, maybe he'd even ask her to marry him. . . .

That night Andrea rushed home from a

late meeting at the office. She had told Jim to meet her at her apartment at eight thirty, and as she hurried through her lobby she glanced at her watch and saw it was eight forty-five. Damn.

When she got out of the elevator Jim was there waiting in the hallway as he once had so many nights ago. *Thank God he came that night,* she said to herself. What would have come of the relationship if he hadn't?

"Sorry," she said, kissing him and getting her keys out. "Have you been here long?"

"No," he lied. "I just got here." He wanted the evening to go smoothly: no hitches and no slip-ups. What did waiting a few minutes mean anyway?

"Good," she said. "Things were just a mess at the office."

A few moments later, as they sat on the couch with drinks, Jim turned to Andrea and smiled. He had a wonderful gleam in his eye, a spark that she loved, and she smiled too. "You look happy," she said. "What happened? Did you have a good class with Olga?"

"Yeah, I did, actually, but that's not what I'm smiling about."

"Tell me!" she said, snuggling up to him. "I could use some good news."

He grinned. "Okay. How does this sound? White sand beaches, blue sky and turquoise water, a casino if you want it, but all the privacy in the world if you want that."

"It sounds wonderful. Like paradise. Why are you taunting me though?"

"It's not a taunt; it's next weekend. For the two of us. I've gotten us tickets and booked a reservation for us on Paradise Island. Four days and four nights at the Brittannia Hotel."

"Four days?"

"Sure. We'll leave Friday night and come back on Tuesday. You can be back at work Tuesday afternoon."

She bit her lip. "Jim, I can't."

"What?"

"It's a wonderful idea and I can't tell you how great I think it is that you planned this, but I just can't miss Monday; I have a really important meeting with some producers who are flying in just to meet me."

"Can't Sloan handle it?"

"I guess he could, but it's my project. I wouldn't want him to."

For a moment Jim stared into her eyes. His own were unreadable. Then he reached into his pocket for a cigarette and lit it. "I see," he finally said, so quietly she had barely heard him.

He didn't want to look at her. What was it Lynda Palmer had said? That all decisions would inevitably fall to Andrea to make, that he'd have no power or independence. He had argued with Lynda; but had she been right?

"Jim?" Andrea said quietly. "Look, why don't we just make it for another time? We can plan it together and then we can be sure I don't have any meetings or anything."

"Ah. I see. We can plan it together," he repeated tonelessly. "And we can make sure you don't have any commitments, since naturally I wouldn't, right?"

"I didn't mean —"

"I think you did," he cut in. "And I think you really can't take the fact that someone else can ever make a decision. It all has to be in your hands, doesn't it?"

"Jim, you just don't understand what I'm telling you. I want to go; I'd *love* to go. I just can't go this weekend."

He shook his head. "It has nothing to do with this weekend or next weekend or the weekend after, Andrea. I was talking to someone the other day who said certain things about managers. I defended you because I love you. But I wonder whether she was right."

"What? Jim, who? What did she say?"

"It's not important," he said quietly. He took a last drag of his cigarette and stubbed it out, then stood up from the couch.

"Jim?"

"I have a lot of thinking to do," he said gruffly. He picked up his drink and drained it, then turned and looked at Andrea with ice-blue eyes. "The Bill Stephenson show is still set for tomorrow, isn't it?"

"Yes. But Jim —"

"Call me if there are any changes in the schedule," he said coolly. And he walked out the door.

Andrea couldn't believe it. What had just happened? Jim's reaction had been frightening — cold and sudden and mystifying.

Had she been wrong? Should she have tried to change her schedule around?

But that wasn't what his anger had been about. Jim had even said he wasn't talking about the weekend; it had only been the igniting spark for something that ran much deeper.

Obviously he had been offended because

she hadn't been able to say yes. He had planned something secretly, optimistically, romantically and on his own, and she had turned him down. And now he was reacting as if she had rejected him completely.

She sighed. Who was it who had planted the seeds of doubt in his mind? Of course, she couldn't really blame anyone else — you didn't get talked into doubting the strength of a relationship by a third party unless you already doubted it somewhere deep inside. And she had always known from the beginning that Jim would be rubbed the wrong way by certain aspects of her position.

What worried her most was that he didn't seem to trust her anymore; he didn't seem to believe in her or in the love they had proclaimed for each other. His reaction seemed to be another aspect of the jealousy that had been plaguing him; and she wondered when, if ever, he would come to realize how wrong he was. There was nothing that could destroy an otherwise good relationship as easily as mistrust, she felt. And Jim seemed to be victim to a bad case of it.

And she had no idea how to change the situation. How could she change it when she wasn't its true cause?

The next morning Andrea went in to talk to Sloan about it. She wanted to call Jim to ask if he was all ready for the Bill Stephenson show he'd be taping in the afternoon, but every time she had reached for the phone she had frozen, terrified of what she might hear if she called him.

"You've got to call him because you're his manager," Sloan said firmly. "Now, come on, Andrea. I don't have to tell you that."

She sighed. "Well, *you* could call."

He smiled. "The tigress of the management world and she can't call her boyfriend. You're losing it, kid."

"Sloan, this is serious!"

"I'm being serious. You can call him and be straightforward. Ask him if he's set for the show, then ask him about last night." He shrugged. "I really think that's all you can do."

Andrea knew she had to take Sloan's advice. It was her obligation to talk to Jim before he was going to tape a show, and she would have felt silly handing the job over to Sloan. But she knew Jim better than Sloan did. She went back to her office, sat down at the desk, and reached for the phone. Then a horrible feeling of cold dread overcame her and made her dizzy. Her fingers were numb and her palms were wet, and her stomach suddenly felt as if she had drunk ten cups of coffee this morning. She was scared. A voice inside told her to wait, not to call.

But she dialed, and she waited, and then she heard his voice.

Her heart skipped.

"Hi, Jim. It's Andrea," she said unnecessarily.

Silence.

"Um, I was wondering if you were ready for the Bill Stephenson show. I mean if you —" Damn. She had been going to say *if you need any advice*. But he seemed so wildly sensitive about his independence these days. "If you need anything," she finally finished.

"It isn't show-and-tell, is it? I thought I would just bring myself."

"Well, yes. I just meant —"

"I'll be fine."

There was a silence, an awful silence in which she wanted to ask him why: Why was he throwing their relationship away? Why was he destroying the most beautiful thing she had ever experienced? Why couldn't he trust her?

She remembered how when he had first told her he loved her he had made her promise she wouldn't let him ruin the relationship. She had been confused back then; why would he ruin it? And he had seemed convinced he would, that inevitably he would destroy it, which went along with what Sloan had said about him — it would be impossible for him to learn to trust.

But that wasn't fair! She loved him so much.

"Um, what . . ." she finally began falteringly. "Did you decide anything about last night? I mean about the tickets?"

"I canceled them this morning," he said quietly.

"Jim, I —"

"Look, Andrea, I'd like to work with Sloan from now on."

"What?"

"I'm sure you can work it out. Just . . . just tell him I'll talk to him after the Bill Stephenson show."

"Jim —"

"I have to start getting ready. Good-bye, Andrea."

He hung up before she even had a chance to say goodbye.

She spent the morning in tears, unable

to believe that the beautiful joy she had come to take for granted was no longer hers. It was all over. Done. Finished.

It was almost as if Jim had been looking for an excuse, as if he had picked a fight just to get out of the relationship.

But a part of her screamed *No! He loved you. You know that and you can never doubt it.*

And she knew, deep in her heart, that he had loved her, that he loved her still. But with him, love obviously wasn't enough.

She couldn't believe it was over. All the plans she had made. . . . And though she had called some of them fantasies, that had been a smokescreen for the truth. They weren't idle daydreams; they were fervent hopes, plans. And now she'd have to forget them, to put them aside perhaps forever.

And she was powerless to change the situation. She hadn't done anything to lead Jim to change his feelings, so she could do nothing now. As his love for her had deepened, his trust and faith had grown shallower until they dried up completely. And now he intended to let their love die.

Jim spoke to Sloan, as promised, later that afternoon, and Sloan came in to tell

Andrea that he would be taking care of Jim's business from now on.

"It'll be better this way," he said gently. "You may find it helps speed things along."

"There's nothing to be sped," she said glumly. "I know it's over and I know there's no way I can change his mind."

"We'll see," Sloan assured her. "We'll see."

Andrea took Sloan's optimism as a sign of hope. Maybe he had sensed something in Jim's voice, maybe Jim had even spoken to him privately about her. But she soon found, as the days passed and turned to weeks, as fall lapsed into gray winter, that she had been wrong. And her pain remained deep.

Jim didn't come to the office at all during those first few weeks; by tacit agreement he and Sloan had begun meeting at La Fourchette, or even at the coffee shop in the lobby. For Andrea this seemed worse than having to see him in the hallways of Hammond/Sutton, which she had expected and geared herself up for. It was so painful to think she was back to hearing about Jim and seeing him only from afar, as if their love had never existed.

His career had taken off at rocket speed. The Kropotkins signed him to a three-picture deal, and Sloan was constantly sending him to auditions for Broadway and off-Broadway plays. Olga Rafelson sang his praises endlessly to Andrea, and she heard good things about his acting from other clients of hers who were in Rafelson's class. But Andrea never saw him.

And then at seven thirty one evening in November, Andrea was leaving the office. She looked up and saw Jim coming down the hall.

For a split-second, she had a chance to see him without his seeing her. He looked tired and a bit thinner, but he was the man she loved, and the sight of him brought tears to her eyes and constricted her throat. He was paler than he had been in October, but the darkness of five o'clock shadow shaded his face, and his dark wavy hair was a bit longer. But he was the same man she missed so much.

And then he looked up and saw her. He looked astonished, as if the thought had never crossed his mind that he'd see her if he came to the office. His gait slowed but continued, and when he came to within a yard of her, he said, "Hello, Andrea," in a quiet, different voice. The leathery huskiness was still there, but there was so much uncertainty. . . .

"Hi, Jim."

She followed his gaze and realized what he was looking at. She was wearing the pendant he had gotten her from Tiffany's — the day all the jealousy had begun in earnest — and his gaze traveled from the pendant to her eyes. He was silently questioning her, and he seemed surprised, very surprised, that she was wearing it.

For a moment they reached each other. She was on the brink of saying, I can't go on like this; he was on the brink of saying, Do you think we could start over?

But neither one could do anything but look into the other's eyes.

And then Jim said, "Sloan's still here, right?"

"Yes, of course," she answered.

He nodded. "Good. We have an appointment. Obviously." For a moment there was the hint of the self-mocking smile she had loved so much. He knew he was muddled, and he seemed almost ready to laugh at their joint awkwardness. But the near smile faded then, and all he said was, "Well, I'll see you."

"Right."

And he walked past her down the hall.

A few minutes later, as he sat with Sloan in his office, he was only half-listening when Sloan said, "Jim, our appointment with Danforth is at nine tomorrow morning. This is serious because up until now Danforth was sure that Owen's lawyers weren't really going to go through with this."

"Then why did they start it?"

Sloan sighed. "You really haven't been listening, have you, pal? There are nuisance suits like this all the time. I'm sure Carson-Cahill, Owen's lawyers, thought that we'd settle quickly in order to stay out of court, and they'd get some nice profitable fraction of the ten million. That's what we thought they were after anyway. Only now the trial date is two weeks away, and they show no signs of not going through with it."

Jim said nothing. Then he looked at Sloan and asked, "Is Andrea seeing anyone right now?"

Sloan sighed. He obviously wasn't going to get through to Jim at all this evening. "No, she's not, Jim. She wasn't when you were seeing her and she isn't now."

"It's funny," Jim mused. "So many things that bothered me when Andrea and I were together seem so much less

important than . . . than anything else."
For a few moments he said nothing. Then he turned to Sloan and said, "All right, let's get to work. We have a lot to get through."

As Sloan continued to go over the finer details of Owen's sins, he wondered whether Jim could possibly be thinking of trying to reconcile with Andrea. For weeks now he himself had realized he had been unfair: he had been jealous, a dog in the manger uninterested in the woman but unwilling to see anyone else make her happy. Seeing how happy she and Jim truly were had snapped him back to his senses. And now he hoped that Jim could make her happy once again. But it was hard to say whether that would ever happen. Jim didn't want to even discuss Andrea for more than a few seconds.

Andrea left the office wishing she hadn't seen Jim but playing the incident over and over again in her mind. She had known, of course, that she'd eventually have to see him, that the time would come when they would stand face to face once again. But she hadn't ever been sure, until now, that so much would still be there in his eyes, in his voice, in the love that seemed to be struggling to break free. She had always worn the pendant as a symbol for herself, as an acknowledgment that she wouldn't pretend their love had never existed, even if Jim were willing to deny it. And now, this evening, she had seen in his eyes that the love was there for him as well. Yet, she couldn't be sure that he had even acknowledged it to himself. He had tasted it, grown frightened of losing it, and thrown it away forever.

She thought about calling him. She had thought about it hundreds, maybe thousands of times. But it held the potential for too much danger, too much hurt. She was beginning to get over the pain, and she was leading her life better than she would have thought was possible under the circumstances. And if she began seeing him, she had to be sure he wouldn't hurt her in the same way all over again. If he wasn't ready to acknowledge what she meant to him and that he wanted to try to work their problems out, there was no point in even speaking with him. All it could do was hurt.

Secretly she thought he would call that night. She couldn't forget the look in his eyes, and she couldn't forget the silent questioning, perhaps the wrestling with himself. Yet, the side that had been fighting for her had obviously lost. He didn't call.

The next morning Sloan told her that Jim had been very preoccupied with her the evening before, and that he thought that seeing her had really shaken Jim up. "I think he will call you," Sloan said. "Really."

Andrea grimaced. "You know what? I half hope he doesn't. If he's so unwilling to try to even explore what's going on, then what's the point? Tell me what's going on with the suit. That's all I really want to know."

"It looks bad," Sloan said. "Owen's team is going full steam ahead. Danforth has been doing his best to be threatening without specifying what we have on Owen, but it hasn't worked so far."

"Why hasn't he been specific?" Andrea asked. "Wouldn't that be more effective?"

Sloan shrugged. "I guess he's saving it. Anyway, they do seem to be ready to go to court."

"Then I think Danforth is going about this all wrong," Andrea said. "It would be insane for Jim to have to spend even one minute in a courtroom for that suit. And look, wasn't Danforth the one who said we were going to get down into the dirt with Owen? Where's the dirt? He should have told Owen's lawyers *weeks* ago that Owen's a lying cheat and that not only are we going to expose him, but we're going to take him for everything he's got if we have to."

Sloan hesitated. Then he said, "You know, I think you're right. I don't know what the hell Danforth's doing. I'm going to give him a call. We're the clients, right? We have a say."

Andrea smiled. "Hey, watch that. Those are dangerous words!"

Sloan laughed. "That's the first time I've seen you smile in weeks, kid. Keep it up."

She winked. "I'm going to try."

But she wasn't able to free herself. She worked, and she worked well, but she ached deep inside; she missed Jim so much. And she was plagued with the notion that she wasn't doing the right thing, that perhaps all Jim needed was one phone call, and that if she didn't follow through, he would be lost to her forever, certain that he had been right to mistrust her.

Andrea was proven right in one area. A week before Owen's suit was set to go to trial, Sloan got a jubilant call from Charles

Danforth. Carson-Cahill had backed down completely and withdrawn their suit, having advised their client he'd be lucky if Jim didn't sue *him* at this point. Wisely they had always advised Owen not to let loose with the torrent of negative publicity he had wanted to release about Jim. Now, though, when they heard how many specific instances of fraud Jim was prepared to sue Owen for, they not only withdrew the complaint, but they then let Owen go as a client, washing their hands of him completely.

But it was a bittersweet moment for Andrea when Sloan told her of the news. She was lonely, damn it. She missed Jim. That was what she cared about — not some lawsuit, even if it had been for all the money in the world.

Her clients during this period all did beautifully, since Andrea had thrown herself into her work and tried not to get distracted by her emotions. Lorenzo and Marina were her two favorites, and though she wasn't all that close to either, she spent a lot of time with both.

One day, as she was leaving the office with Lorenzo, Sloan and Jim came down the hall in the other direction.

Andrea stopped for a moment. In all the

time since that meeting in the hallway, she hadn't seen Jim even once. And her first thought after she saw how wonderful he looked was that she was with Lorenzo, the man he had been so jealous about.

They all nodded and said muted hellos, though Andrea's and Jim's gazes caught and held. And then they passed, the corridors silent once more.

That night Andrea felt wildly restless, like a wild mare suddenly confined. Everything felt wrong. Her life, on the surface, was as smooth as glass; her job was great, she had good friends, she had a good future in many areas. But today she had seen the man she loved, and they had barely spoken. How could she live her life knowing the relationship had ended unjustly?

Yet, whenever she had asked herself that question before, she had come back to the same sad answer. Until Jim felt their love was worth fighting for, until he could see that he was wrong and that trust was his to cherish, their love could never last. It was up to him to see that; she had done all she could.

She got ready for bed early, taking a long hot bath and then wrapping herself in a thick white terry robe. She was suddenly exhausted, the emotional tension of the day and evening having drained her quickly and forcefully once she had faced the truth. Now sleep would be welcome. If she could sleep.

At eleven thirty the phone rang, and she woke with a start.

"Hello?"

"Andrea?"

She swallowed and closed her eyes. It was Jim.

"Andrea?"

"Yes. Hi."

"I have to see you," he said quietly. "I know it's late — maybe in more ways than one. But I have to see you tonight."

"Where —"

"I'm right at the corner. I left my apartment and I was going to go to your place, but then I thought . . ." His voice trailed off. "Anyway, can I come up?"

She hesitated. More than anything in the world she wanted to see him. She loved him; she knew he didn't want to come over in order to say some sort of final goodbye. If he was coming, it was because he wanted her back. But could she trust him? Could she trust in his desire to make it work? And could she trust herself to say no if she saw that was the only sensible response?

"All right, come," she said quietly. "I'll be here."

The minutes seemed endless as she waited. She had no idea what she'd do, what she'd say, if she'd have any way of judging what he was going to say. If he had told her right there in the hallway at the office that he wanted her back, in front of Sloan and Lorenzo and completely out of the blue, would she have said anything but yes? And was that wrong? How could you say no to the person you loved more than anyone in the world, to the person you *knew* you were made for?

Suddenly he was there. She heard the slam of the elevator doors, and she ran to the door and opened it.

And the moment she saw Jim's face she knew she could never say no to him. Not if he was willing to try again. . . .

He smiled as he came forward. "Do you know how good it feels to see you and say something more than hello?" He came up to where she stood and looked at her in wonder. "I had some sense knocked into me today and I just hope it isn't too late."

"Come on in," she said quietly. She had to wait and see, to see if she had been right, if maybe dreams could come true.

He stepped in and put his hands on her shoulders. "Just to touch you," he murmured. "Andrea —" He sighed. "Andrea, I've made the biggest mistake of my life. I don't know where to start, really, except to tell you that I went wild today." He smiled. "Your friend Sloan is a good guy."

She smiled. "Yes, he is."

He took her hand, and for a moment she closed her eyes under the warmth of his touch, a warmth she had missed so much. And slowly he led her down into the living room and over to the window, where the lights of the city glimmered like stars on the waters of the East River.

"I've been trying to think of the right way to say this, so that you'll believe me," he said softly. "You know, when we fell in love, or when I fell in love with you, I used to worry late at night over what you thought of some of the things you had read about me. I loved you, and even though I hadn't planned for it to happen, once it had, I didn't want to ruin it. And I'd look back at things I had said, like that men weren't made to be with just one woman, that kind of thing."

She smiled. "Mmm. I remember."

"Well, those were all true at one time.

And I thought, She'll never think I'm really right for her. But you seemed to be willing to forget my past." He paused.

"I was," she said quietly. "I did forget, Jim."

He sighed. "I wish . . . well, I wish I had been able to. I suddenly thought you had to be the way I used to be. I thought I'd never be able to trust you. And today, when I saw you with Lorenzo, at first I went wild. Sloan told me I had nothing to worry about, that there was nothing between the two of you. And I thought to myself, You can't rely on what someone else says. You have to believe it yourself."

"And do you?" she asked softly.

"What I believe," he said slowly, "is that I've never loved anyone as much as I love you, Andrea. I've never had these feelings — this jealousy — before, because I've never felt this way before. And maybe someday I won't even be jealous. But there's one thing I know, Andrea. I don't want to be apart from you anymore. I can live with some bad feelings because I don't want to ever give you up." His eyes seemed to be questioning her, asking her if he should go on, asking her if she still loved him. "I just hope . . ." He sighed. "There are things I've learned lately. I think about what's valuable, and what's worth fighting for in this life. I helped Kate get a job through an old friend of mine. It meant making up with someone I had held a grudge against for about ten years. But I did it for her because she's so important to me. And there have been other things lately. You were only trying to help me with my career and you would never do anything to hurt me. I realize that now. What do you say we try it again?" He looked out at the lights on the river and then into Andrea's eyes.

"Jim, if it's working out with Sloan, why don't we leave it as it is?" As she looked into his eyes she felt that this decision was best for both of them, though she wasn't sure it was what he wanted to hear.

"Okay, if you think it'll make things easier, but I have to know," he said softly. "I can tell you because I want you to know. Other people may have more than one love, Andrea; they may meet two or three or four people in their lives who mean everything to them. But I know that with me, you're the one. That you'll always be the one. And I have to know . . ."

"Oh, Jim, I love you," she said softly. "I've loved you since . . . maybe since we first made love. Maybe before then. I never stopped loving you. But I didn't think it could work."

"Anything can work if there's enough love, darling," he said, taking her in his arms, "I know it's true. I just know it. And we can make it true."

"Do you really think — ?"

"I know it, Andrea. And I know we can do anything and everything if we're together, if we make it real." His gaze melted into hers. "If you'll be my wife," he whispered.

His words sounded more beautiful than she had ever imagined. And she knew that he was right, that together they could do anything, conquer any fears or doubts or uncertainties . . . if they were together.

And she whispered, "Yes, yes, yes," before he drew her into the loveliest and happiest embrace of her life.

We hope you have enjoyed this Large Print book. Other Thorndike Press or Chivers Press Large Print books are available at your library or directly from the publishers.

For more information about current and upcoming titles, please call or write, without obligation, to:

Publisher
Thorndike Press
295 Kennedy Memorial Drive
Waterville, ME 04901
Tel. (800) 223-1244

OR

Chivers Press Limited
Windsor Bridge Road
Bath BA2 3AX
England
Tel. (0225) 335336

All our Large Print titles are designed for easy reading, and all our books are made to last.